First Job

by Jane Sorenson

illustrated by Kathleen L. Smith

STANDARD PUBLISHING
Cincinnati, Ohio   24-03961

All Scripture quotations are from the *Holy Bible: New International Version,* © 1973, 1984 by the International Bible Society. Used by permission of Zondervan Bible Publishers and the International Bible Society.

LIBRARY OF CONGRESS
Library of Congress Cataloging-in-Publication Data

Sorenson, Jane.
    First job!/by Jane Sorenson; illustrated by Kathleen L. Smith.
        p. cm.–(Katie Hooper book; 5)
    Summary: Katie and Sara babysit to earn money for skis until Sara discovers that God has other moneymaking plans for her.
    ISBN 0-87403-561-9
    [1. Baby sitters–Fiction. 2. Moneymaking projects–Fiction. 3. Friendship–Fiction. 4. Christian life–Fiction.] I. Smith, Kathleen L., 1950- ill. II. Title. III. Series: Sorenson, Jane. Katie Hooper book; 5.
PZ7.S7214Fj 1989   89-4546
[Fic]–dc19   CIP
                                                                      AC

To two very special sisters

Margaret Volle
and
Julia Volle Gernand

with love and thanks to God
for all they have brought into my life

The First Snowfall

I woke up smiling. Ever since I won that award at school, I've been having stupid dreams. This time, our principal, Mr. Hobbs, was hanging a medal around my neck. "Congratulations, Katie Hooper," he said. "You've been chosen 'Citizen of the World'!" As people cheered, I smelled something. And when I looked down, I realized that hanging from the ribbon around my neck was a hamburger from Burger King!

Because my room was so cold, I dressed fast. I hardly noticed the white dusting of snow outside my window.

"You don't seem very excited, Katie," Mom said when I came into the kitchen. "I can remember when the first snowfall almost sent you into orbit!"

"Oh, Mom!" I said. "That was when I was little." I watched her spoon cereal into my sister's tiny mouth. "Maybe next year Amy will get all hyper when it snows."

Mom smiled. "I sure hope so! I'll have to admit that my heart beat faster when I first looked out the window this morning!"

I looked up from my oatmeal and grinned. "But Mom, this hardly covers the ground!"

"I know. But just wait!"

I remembered something. "Is there any chance we could get more snow? Don't forget, we're going up to Divide tomorrow!"

"I haven't forgotten," Mom told me. "I can't wait to see what Mayblossom McDuff has done with our cabin!"

"Do you think she's changed it?"

"I don't know," Mom said. "Even if she hasn't, I'm sure it will look different. Every house changes when new people move in."

"I believe it! At least this place sure did!" I glanced around the kitchen. "It doesn't seem possible that Home Sweet Home used to be vacant, boarded up, and filled with junk!"

"I know," Mom said. "Sometimes I get discouraged because we still have so much to do. But we've accomplished miracles already. I can't believe we've only been here since the end of the summer."

"Some of the kids at the bus stop still call this Spook House!" I giggled. "I think Sara half expects to see the ghost every time she walks by!"

"Now if your father can only do something to get us more heat!" Mom said.

"Where is Dad?"

"He left before dawn. He was hoping to paint the morning light on that first snow."

"I have to go!" I grabbed my jacket. "Can I still bake cookies this afternoon? I'd like to take some to M. tomorrow."

Mom nodded. "Actually, the heat of the oven will feel good in here! By the way, didn't you say Sara wants to learn how to cook? Maybe she'd like to help you."

"I'll ask her," I said. I half expected Mom to tell me to wear boots, but she didn't. So I kicked them back into the pile next to the door. "Bye. I'll see you right after school."

I ran all the way to the bus stop. With every step, the snow blew away under my feet.

As usual, my best friend, Sara Wilcox, was at the bus stop waiting for me. She was practically dancing up and down. I smiled at her. "So what's charging your batteries this morning?"

"You have to ask?" She waved her arm out in a dramatic circle. "Behold!"

9

"The snow?" I said. "You're all hyper about this puny bit of snow? I can't believe it!"

"But this is Colorado!" she announced.

"Thanks for telling me! Didn't they ever have snow in Omaha?"

"Don't be silly, Katie," she said. "But in Omaha we didn't have the Rocky Mountains!"

At that point, Calvin Young and Christopher Bean walked up. "How's my sweetheart this morning?" Calvin asked.

"Knock it off, Calvin," I said. "How come you're so happy?"

"He always looks like this on Friday," Christopher said.

"Wrong!" Calvin said. "It's the snow! It's time to wax the boards! It won't be long now!"

Sara's eyes got big. "You mean you actually ski?" she asked.

"Are you kidding?" Calvin couldn't believe it. "Everybody in Colorado skis!"

"I don't," Christopher said.

"I don't," Sara said.

I didn't say anything. I just waited.

"That's because you both just moved here," Calvin said. "Why, around here, babies wear ski boots instead of booties! Kids snowplow before they crawl!"

Sara looked at me. "Katie doesn't ski," she said.

I played it cool. I grinned. "Someday I might ski. So far I've been so busy, I just haven't tried it yet!"

Calvin grinned back. "Well, darling, don't wait too long! Didn't I tell you, Katie? We're going to Aspen on our honeymoon!"

"That settles it," I laughed. "I can't marry you, Calvin! If I ever get around to skiing, it will be at Vail or Breckenridge!"

Actually, I was faking, and I'm sure Calvin knew it. The places I mentioned are famous Colorado ski areas. I was trying to sound like I know my way around. Sara and Christopher seemed impressed.

"Hey, you guys, stop goofing around and be serious," Christopher said. "I'd really like to try downhill skiing. What's the first thing I should do?"

"Get yourself some skis!" Calvin told him. "And then pray for snow!"

The bus pulled up, and the door flew open. "Let's go!" the driver said.

As usual, the boys sat in the back of the bus, and Sara and I sat together in the front. "Katie, I'm impressed," she said. "If a boy ever talked about marrying me, I'd just die! How can you be so cool?"

"Calvin's just teasing," I told her. "He's been talking like that ever since kindergarten. I

11

think it's just because my birthday's on Valentine's Day."

"But do you like him?"

"Calvin? Oh, he's all right."

"I mean, is he your boyfriend?"

"Who, Calvin?" I laughed. "Don't be dumb, Sara! I've never had a boyfriend."

Her eyes got big. "Well, if you ever do get one, will you tell me?"

"Of course," I said. "But don't hold your breath."

I guess it was bound to happen. All day it was hard to concentrate on school. Off and on I kept thinking about snow. Until now, I've lived in a cabin in the country. I wondered what it will be like to spend a winter in town. I certainly hope it won't be boring!

"All day long I've been thinking about skiing," Sara said, when we got on the bus after school. "I think we should try it."

"There's only one problem," I told her.

"My coordination?"

"No, that's not it," I said. "Money, Sara. Skiing takes a lot of money. Dad says it's a sport for rich people."

"That's why you don't ski?"

"Bingo!" I said. "When your father earns money by painting pictures of mountains, you don't do a lot of things!"

"But I thought you said he's illustrating books."

"He is," I said. "But even that isn't the kind of job where he gets paid every week. We still have to depend on the Lord for money."

"I don't know what you're talking about!"

Since Sara's just learning about Jesus, I tried to be patient. "It's kind of hard to explain," I admitted. "But the Lord knows what we need, and we pray about it, and He takes care of it by sending a job or something."

"Katie, do you think the Lord could help us get skis?" she asked.

"Sure—if He wants us to have them!"

"Why wouldn't He?"

"I don't know," I said. "Maybe He knows we'd fall and break our legs or something."

Sara sighed. "This is getting too complicated! Can't we leave accidents out of it?"

"I was just trying to answer your question!"

"Then I'm sorry I asked," she said. "Maybe we should just figure out how to earn some money. There has to be a way!"

I laughed. I've heard that before! That's what Sara always says! But then I really started thinking about it. "Sara, I think you were right the first time!" I told her. "Since the Lord wants us to depend on Him, He probably wants us to ask Him."

She looked over at me. "Well, do you want to do it, or do I have to?"

Actually, sometimes I do pray silently at school. But, to tell the truth, I've never once prayed out loud while riding on a school bus! If that's chicken, I'm guilty!

"It's pretty noisy," I told her. "Why don't we just wait and pray when we get to my house."

Sara and I
Bake Cookies

By the time we got to my house, Sara and I forgot all about praying. In fact, we even forgot all about snow and skiing.

"Are you sure you've never made chocolate chip cookies?" I asked. It hardly seemed possible.

"I'm positive," she said. "Katie, I'm going to tell you a secret. The most time I've spent in any kitchen is right here in yours!"

"But we've never even cooked anything together," I said.

She grinned. "That's right!"

Just then Mom walked in. "Hi, girls! All set for some baking?"

"All set!" Sara said.

Mom smiled at me. "Do you want my help?"

"No offense," I said, "but we can handle it."

"I'll be in the family room." Mom turned to leave.

"We'll give you a sample when we're done," Sara promised. "They're going to be the best cookies you've ever tasted!"

"If you've never cooked before, how can you be so confident?" I asked.

Sara grinned. "I don't know. How hard can it be?"

I knew we were in big trouble as soon as I handed Sara an apron.

"What's this?"

"It's an apron!" I said. "You don't want to get your school clothes dirty!"

"If you're going to insult me, this is never going to work!" Sara said.

I relaxed and smiled at her. "I take it you don't usually wear an apron."

"Maybe today will be different," she admitted. "Opening the refrigerator doesn't exactly wreck your clothes. And neither does pushing the timer on a microwave!"

"Oh, my," I said. I sounded just like my mother. I tried to remember how Mom first taught me to cook. But it was so long ago! I took a deep breath. "The first thing we have to do is read the recipe."

"Right," Sara said. "And that's as far as I ever get!"

"What do you mean?"

"At my house, we never have the things on the list! Every time I get inspired to cook something, the recipe always includes something we don't have—like corn syrup. Or something I've never heard of—like nutmeg or *thy me.*" She said it slowly.

I tried to figure out what she was talking about. Then I grinned. "Sara, it isn't *thy me!* It's pronounced *time!*"

"Whatever," she said.

We worked together. While she read off the ingredients, I pulled them out and set them on the table.

"Flour. Salt. Soda."

"Stop right there," she said. "That's soda?"

I handed her the box, and she started to laugh. "I thought it came in a bottle! You know, like Coke or Pepsi. At least that's what my grandmother always called it."

I shook my head. "When a recipe says *soda,* it means *baking soda.*"

"No wonder I got confused!" Sara looked down at the recipe. "Next comes granulated sugar." After watching me get out the canister, Sara looked inside. "Katie, this just looks like plain old sugar to me! What makes it so special?"

18

"It is plain old sugar," I told her.

She put her hands on her hips. "And how was I supposed to know that?"

"Beats me! I don't really know," I said.

"Next comes oatmeal."

I reached up and set a round box on the table.

"Stop! Hold the phone!" she said. "That's oatmeal?"

I pulled open the top. "This is what it looks like before you cook it," I said.

"Amazing!" she said. "When we had it, it never looked like that! Can you cook this without a microwave oven?"

"I can't believe it," I said. "I've never heard of cooking oatmeal in an oven!"

Once we had assembled everything, I showed Sara how to sift the dry ingredients. "So that's how you measure salt!" she laughed. "I never could figure out how to shake it into that little spoon!"

I laughed too. "Sara, Sara," I said. "You could go on the stage!"

"I've thought about it," she said. "OK, now what's an unbeaten egg?"

I just looked at her. "You don't know how to beat an egg?"

"I guess I've never tried," she said. "What's the prize, anyhow?"

I started laughing again. And this time I

couldn't stop. That got Sara going, and we both laughed so hard that Mom heard us and came in to see what was happening.

"Tell Mom what you just said!" I gasped.

Soon Mom was laughing too. Neither of us had ever thought about how cooking terms might sound to somebody who never cooks.

At last we calmed down. Mom left, and I demonstrated how to break an egg.

"So that's how it's done!" Sara said. "Can I try the other one?"

Somehow, I knew what would come next. And it happened just as I expected. We spent the next five minutes picking pieces of egg shell out of our batter!

"I'm sorry!" Sara said.

"Don't worry about it," I told her. "Actually, you did great for the first time!"

A few minutes later, the dough itself was all mixed. We took turns trying to blend in the nuts and chocolate chips. The nuts were easy, but we had to be careful because the chocolate chips kept flying out of the bowl!

"Now we have to turn on the oven," I said. I showed her how to set it for 375. "Is this anything like a microwave oven?"

"It's a lot bigger," Sara told me. "Does this thing get hot?"

"You're kidding!"

"No, I'm not," she said. "Our microwave oven never even gets warm!"

"You're putting me on!"

"Maybe you should come over to *my* kitchen sometime," Sara said. "I'll teach you to cook a hot dog!"

"It's a deal," I said.

I started to show Sara how to space the balls of cookie dough two inches apart on the cookie sheet. "You don't have to grease it," I told her. "Mom has a saying: *It's a poor cookie that can't grease its own bottom!*"

Sara laughed. "Where did she learn that?"

"From *her* mother."

"And I suppose you'll teach that to *your* children," Sara said.

"Sure," I said. "But first I'm teaching it to you!"

"Just one more question," Sara said. "How come you're pushing the dough off the spoon with your fingers?"

"They're clean," I said.

"But you aren't following the recipe," she said. "It says to *drop* it by teaspoons!"

Then I really started to laugh. I could just picture the two of us standing on chairs and aiming spoonfuls of dough down at a cookie sheet! I couldn't wait to tell Mom!

We set the timer for eight minutes and waited.

Wow, did those cookies smell fantastic! Afterwards, it was tough letting them cool a minute after we took them out of the oven.

"Best I ever ate!" Sara announced. "Hey, if it's OK, I'd like to take some home. Wait until I tell my mother I made them. She'll freak out!"

"Sure! Take enough for supper," I said. "In fact, why don't you copy down the recipe? Then you can bake cookies whenever you feel like it."

Sara didn't say anything. She just stood there and grinned. "Actually, I'm getting an idea. Maybe we could make cookies and sell them!" Suddenly, she started dancing around the kitchen. "Katie, that's it! That's how we can earn money for our skis!"

Dollars and Sense

Not to brag, but I'm getting smarter. By now I've learned that Sara gets a lot of ideas. And they don't all turn out to be as wonderful as they first sound!

While I watched my friend dance around the kitchen, I thought back to our school's recent candy sale. Sure, I'll admit that we both won prizes. But the time I spent selling candy got me into an awful jam with my homework! So I knew I had to be careful this time!

"Sara, there's just one problem," I said. "You probably didn't realize it. But I'm not really very good at selling things!"

Sara stopped dancing and grinned at me. "I realized it," she said.

"Oh." I didn't know whether to feel relieved or insulted.

"Katie, when you start a business, everybody doesn't have to be good at everything! I can handle the sales!"

"So, I guess that means I get to bake the cookies?"

"Somebody has to do it," she said. "And you really are better at cooking."

"Thanks." I thought a minute. "Who would buy them?"

"I'm not exactly sure," Sara said. "Give me a break! After all, I just thought up the idea."

Just then my brother Jason walked in. "Hey, something smells good! All right!" As he walked past, he picked up two cookies.

"Stop right there, Jason," Sara said. "Is that the best cookie you've ever eaten or what?"

Jason stood there and ate a bite. "They taste just the same as always." He looked at me. "Oh, did you make these, Katie?"

"We both did," I said. "Sara and I."

He smiled at Sara. "Congratulations!"

She smiled back. "How much would you say a cookie like that is worth?"

"You don't really expect me to pay for it!" he said.

"Of course not!" Sara said. "You know. It's a hypothetical question."

"Beats me!" Jason said. "I've never bought a cookie in my entire life."

"We're thinking about going into business," Sara told him.

"We might do it," I said.

"Who will pay for the ingredients?" Jason asked.

"I knew there was a catch!" I said.

"You can't expect Mom to buy all the groceries and then let you keep all the money," he said.

"Certainly not!" Sara said. "We'd never expect that!"

"Thanks a lot, Jason," I said. "You've given us something to think about!"

"My pleasure!" He paused in the doorway into the dining room. "By the way, did I get any phone calls?"

I just looked at him. He gets about as many phone calls as I do—zilch! "None since we've been home."

"Thanks," he said. "I'll check with Mom."

"I wonder who would call him?" I asked.

"Maybe it's a girl!" Sara said.

"I doubt it. The only time I ever saw my brother with a girl was last summer at the auction barn."

Sara looked at me. "Tell me something, Katie. Be honest! Do you think your brother could go for me?" She began to strut around the table.

I giggled. "No offense, but I doubt it."

With her red hair poking out in every direction, Sara looked just like a bantam rooster. Suddenly, she stopped strutting and became serious. "You're probably right, Katie. I suppose I'm kind of young for him!"

"Don't feel bad. I'm sure Jason likes you," I said. "Sara, how come all of a sudden you're always talking about boyfriends?"

"What do you mean *always?*"

"That's twice today," I said. "The first time was this morning on the bus."

"Twice isn't always!" Sara said. "But I bet you anything Jason's expecting a call from a girl!"

"I never bet!" I told her.

"I figured as much," she said. "And in one way, it's too bad! That rules out getting skis by winning the lottery! I guess we'll just have to sell cookies!"

I tried to think. "Maybe we can come up with another idea," I said. "But for now, we'd better just finish baking these cookies!"

We each started putting dough onto a cookie sheet. I was faster.

"How much is your allowance?" Sara asked suddenly.

A chocolate chip fell off a cookie, and I stuck it back into the dough. "It isn't exactly an allowance," I said slowly. "It's mostly milk money."

"How much?" she asked again.

I told her.

"I can't believe it!" she said. "I got more than that back when I was in kindergarten! What do you do for spending money?"

"I don't know," I said. "It's never really been much of a problem. I guess if I really needed something bad, Mom would try to help me out."

"Katie, when you do things around the house, do you get paid?"

"Like what?"

"Oh, I don't know. Like cleaning your room. Or doing the dishes."

I grinned. "I don't clean my room all that often."

She grinned back. "So I've noticed."

"But even when I do clean it, I'd never expect to get paid," I said. "Jason's room is spotless. And he's never earned a nickel. He just likes it that way!"

"OK, so that's a bad example," Sara said. "How about the dishes? I notice you don't have a dish-washer."

"Why would we need a dishwasher?" I asked. "Jason and I take turns. One week he washes and I dry. And the next week we trade off."

"And you don't get paid?"

"Of course not!" I said. "And Mom doesn't get paid for cooking dinner either!"

"How about your brother? Does he get an allowance?"

I shook my head. "Not really. But Jason has lots of money saved up. Before we moved into town, he worked at a sheep ranch. But he quit in order to help Dad fix up this house."

To be honest, Sara was super slow at putting drops of dough on the cookie sheet. And she stuck them too far apart. But finally we were able to shove her pan into the oven.

"How about you, Sara?" I asked. "It sounds as if you get an allowance."

"I've been given one for as long as I can remember," she said. "Mom wants me to learn how to handle money."

"Didn't you tell me you had almost $10.00? Did you save that from your allowance?"

"That's how," Sara said. "Actually, I could have had lots more, but I spent it on a two-piece bathing suit. And then I found out that I couldn't swim!"

"It sounds like you're good at saving."

"I'm not just good," Sara said, "I'm great! But it's funny. I can go for weeks and weeks without spending a dime. And then I go out and blow the whole thing!"

"That sounds familiar," I said. "Once I got some money for my birthday. I spent it on something I always wanted. But then I discovered that I really didn't want it after all."

"Learning to handle money isn't as easy as it sounds," Sara said.

"You know Kimberly Harris?" I said. She's the new girl in my room. "I can't believe all the money she carries around!"

"I bet her mother gives it to her," Sara said.

I thought about other girls in my room at school. "Sue Capelleti's the lucky one," I said. "She babysits for her neighbor after school every day."

Sara looked up. "What did you just say?"

"I don't know. That Sue Capelleti's lucky?"

"Cancel plans for a cookie business!" Sara said. "I've got a better idea! We can earn money for skis by babysitting!"

"Who would hire us?" I asked. "Besides, you don't have any experience!"

"How about Amy?" she asked. "Doesn't your baby sister count?"

"I could never ask Mom to pay me for taking care of Amy!"

"But she counts as experience!" Sara said.

"Sara, you've never taken care of Amy," I pointed out. "You only held her once."

"A mere technicality," Sara protested. "We can get experience by practicing on Amy. And then we can try for other jobs!" She was dancing around the room again!

Babysitting! This time I could feel a smile spreading across my face. "You know, maybe you have something, Sara!"

Sara closed her eyes. "I can just feel myself gliding down those mountains!"

I grinned. "Me too," I said. "After all, if Calvin Young can do it, how hard can it be?"

Mealtime at Hoopers'

I have no idea what other families do at mealtimes. I don't even know how our traditions got started. But I do know that we Hoopers don't pray before we eat supper. Instead, we all stand behind our chairs, hold hands, and sing.

Actually, this tradition is one of my favorites! Tonight, as we were singing, Dad squeezed my hand.

Praise God, from whom all blessings flow;
Praise Him, all creatures here below;
Praise Him above, ye heavenly host;
Praise Father, Son, and Holy Ghost! Amen."

As usual, I felt wonderful! Once we sat down, I

could tell that there was more on Dad's mind than macaroni and cheese. He took a deep breath, looked around the table, and smiled his biggest smile. I mean, he absolutely *glowed!*

Mom watched him with pleasure. "Steve, I have a question. When you came down from the mountain, did you happen to bring the Ten Commandments? You look just like Moses!"

"Moses had more hair," Jason said.

Dad's face became stern. In a deep, bass voice he thundered, "Thou shalt honor thy father and mother!"

I giggled.

"Wait until you kids see your father's new painting!" Mom said. "I think it's even better than the one that hung in the bank!"

"All right!" Jason said. "Fame and fortune — here we come!"

"I don't know about that," Dad said. "I was very fortunate. The Lord got me to the scene at just the right time! The light was perfect. As the sun came up, the snow actually glistened!"

"Are you going to hang this one in the bank?" I asked. Last time he did that, somebody bought the painting.

"I'm not sure," Dad said. "Actually, all day I've been thinking about something else. You know, the people at church have been so wonderful to us since we moved to town. I think I'd really like to hang this painting in Fellowship Hall."

"Oh, Steve!" Mom said. "What a wonderful idea! There's that wall above the fireplace! It would be perfect!"

Dad reached for her hand. "Elizabeth!" he said. "How did you know? That's exactly what I had in mind!"

My parents love each other so much that sometimes it looks like they forget they even have children! But I don't mind. Not at all!

I looked over at Jason who was just staring at his macaroni and cheese. Finally, he looked up. "Hey, you two!" he said. "Quit acting like a couple of teenagers!"

"Never!" Dad grinned. "In case you forgot, you kids have a very special mother! And I have a very special wife!"

"I feel so fortunate!" Mom said. "I have such a wonderful family! Isn't the Lord good! And now He's even given us this house with no rent to pay!"

Dad nodded. "The arrangement is a good deal for everybody," he reminded us. "The bank is happy to have somebody living here. Their insurance on the empty building was sky-high!"

"How about the doctor bill?" Jason asked. "Did we get enough money from selling the other painting to pay it?"

"We did—exactly enough," Mom said. "To be

honest, I think the doctor was thrilled! He knew we didn't have much money." She stopped and looked at Jason. "You're mighty curious."

"It's OK," Dad told her. "I think Jason and Katie are getting old enough to know about our finances."

"Then I have another question," my brother said. "How have we paid for what we've done to fix up this place?"

"We had to borrow money from the bank," Dad explained. "But we have plenty of time to pay off the loan."

"Wouldn't this be a good time to try to get ahead?" Jason asked.

"You're thinking about selling the painting, aren't you, Son?" Dad said.

My brother nodded.

"I also think it's a good time to give something special to thank the Lord," Dad said.

"If you say so," Jason replied.

"It's a funny thing," Mom told us. "If you wait until you don't need anything more for yourself, you'll probably never give anything to the Lord!"

"But don't we already give Him a tenth of everything we get?" Jason asked.

"Everything we get already belongs to the Lord," Dad explained. "Actually, He lets us use most of it!"

"I never thought of it that way," Jason said.

"Guess what?" I said. "Sara and I are going to save up for skis."

"They're going to sell chocolate chip cookies," Jason said.

"We are not!"

"You were this afternoon!" he said.

"That's all you know about it!"

"That's enough," Mom said. "Katie, where did this idea come from? I don't think I ever heard you talk about wanting to ski."

"I hope you and Sara are patient," Dad said. "Skiing takes a lot of money. I've always thought of it as a sport for rich people."

I couldn't believe it! They didn't sound at all like my positive family! But it really didn't matter. Right then and there, I decided I don't care if they encourage me or not. Somehow, I just know I'm going to ski!

After we finish eating, Dad always reads from the Bible. And then we all pray. "I have just the verses for tonight!" he said.

Suddenly, the telephone started ringing.

"I'll get it," Jason said.

"No, just let it ring," Dad told him.

"I think it's for me."

"Whoever it is will call back," Mom said.

It was hard to sit there and wait. The phone rang eleven times! Finally, it stopped.

"This is from Matthew chapter 6," Dad said.

"Do not store up for yourselves treasures on earth, where moth and rust destroy, and where thieves break in and steal. But store up for yourselves treasures in heaven, where moth and rust do not destroy, and where thieves do not break in and steal. For where your treasure is, there your heart will be also."

"Is it wrong to save money?" I asked.

"Do you think that's what Jesus is saying?" Dad asked.

The phone began ringing again. This time Dad tried to ignore it, which wasn't easy! "What do you think is the point of what I read?" he yelled.

"The Lord wants us to love Him more than our possessions!" Mom yelled.

"This is ridiculous!" Dad yelled. He stood up and walked over to the phone. "This is Steve Hooper," he said. "I'm sorry, but Jason can't come to the phone right now. Would you like him to call you back?" Dad wrote something down. Then he hung up and came back to the table.

He grinned at Jason. "Well, Son, it sounds as if your life is about to change."

Jason's face turned red.

"Aren't you curious about who called?" Dad asked.

"I ... I think I already know."

"Was it a girl?" I asked. "Sara was positive it was going to be a girl!"

"Sara should mind her own business!" Jason said.

"Steve, let's just pray," Mom said.

Dad smiled and bowed his head. "Thank you, Father, for the many ways you've blessed our family. We don't deserve any of it. But You've provided this home. You've given us food to eat, and work to do, and friends who care for us. You've placed us in such a beautiful part of Your world. Look inside our hearts. We love You, Lord! Amen."

The rest of us said, "Amen."

When I opened my eyes, I looked at Jason. He stood up. "Let's get the dishes done, Katie."

"Are you going to call her back?" I asked.

Jason tried to act real cool. "When I get around to it," he said.

Family Secrets

Life is funny, isn't it? I mean, take my family. I spend time with them every single day of my life. And I think I know them like a book. But once in a while, always when I least expect it, I find out something entirely new!

While we were doing the dishes, Jason was unusually quiet. By the time we got to the pans, I couldn't stand it any longer. "Who is she?"

"Don't be a pest!" he said. "Katie, I was wondering. If you and Sara aren't going to sell cookies, then how are you going to make money?"

"If you tell me, I'll tell you!"

He grinned. "I can wait."

Personally, I was more curious. Since the telephone's in the kitchen, I kind of hung around afterwards putting stuff in the cupboards. But it was no use. Jason hung up his towel and left.

Dad had made a fire in the family room, and that's where I found everybody. He and Mom were reading. Amy was asleep in the corner. My dog, January, was asleep next to the fire. And, as usual, Jason had pulled out his book of crossword puzzles. He works one after supper every single night.

I just love fires! Smiling, I curled up with my feet under me and opened my book. But I couldn't concentrate. Instead of reading, I kept glancing over at my brother.

I'll have to admit that Jason isn't bad looking. All of a sudden, he's nearly as tall as Dad. But Dad is huge. Jason is built more like a pencil! Also, my brother has lots more hair! Now I took a good look at his face. To be honest, it is nearly impossible for me to picture Jason as anybody's boyfriend!

Let me make one thing perfectly clear. I really do love my brother! For all of my life, he's been an important part of it! Until I met Sara Wilcox, Jason was my only friend. He taught me how to play games, and then he always won. He thought up adventures, and then he always got to be Robin Hood.

"Responsibility" is Jason Hooper's middle name! For example, he's the one who gets us to

39

"You made up some goofy reasons!" Dad laughed.

"Maybe things are different now," she said.

"It's funny," Dad said. "I used to hate it when my parents complained about how fast time had gone by. But I feel the same today as I did fifteen years ago!"

"It's hard to believe we're old enough to have a son with a girlfriend!" Mom giggled. "We'll never get old! But Jason's right! I guess sometimes we do still act like a couple of teenagers!"

"Don't ever change!" I told them. "When I see how much you love each other, it makes me feel wonderful."

"Everybody changes," Mom said. "But we'll always love each other. That's what our marriage is all about!"

I looked at the fire. "Can I ask a question? Mom, do you ever miss your family?"

Mom didn't say anything.

"Well, Elizabeth?" Dad asked.

"I'll have to admit it," Mom said slowly. "Sometimes I do miss them. Mostly I wish they could see my beautiful children! But I had to make a choice, and I chose to be here with you. I've never been sorry!"

"I often think about that, Elizabeth," Dad said. His voice sounded kind of strange. "Maybe it wasn't fair to make you choose."

Mom didn't reply. And Dad didn't explain. Somehow I knew I shouldn't say anything either. After several moments of silence, a log burned through and fell.

"I guess I'd better go and get some more wood," Dad said.

Mom cleared her throat. "That reminds me, Steve. The house has been cold all day. You don't suppose there's something wrong with the furnace, do you?"

"I checked it right after we moved in. It looked all right to me," he said. "Isn't it working?"

"It's working, but I'm still cold. Steve, are you sure you understand such an old furnace?"

Dad frowned. "Of course, I'm sure!"

Just then, Jason appeared in the doorway. He was trying hard to look cool. "Well, what are all of you staring at?"

"Who is she?" I asked.

"Yes," Mom said. "We all want to know!"

"If I tell you, will you promise to stay off my back?" he asked.

Dad grinned. "You know we can't really promise that, Son! You might as well realize it. Teasing goes with the territory!"

Jason sat down. "OK, I'll tell you. Her name is Allie Meredith." His face turned red. "It's no big deal. We both just happen to be very interested in the environment!"

43

Dad smiled. "Now I've heard everything!"

"It's the truth!" Jason said. "And it's the last time I'll ever tell you guys anything!"

"I'm going out to get wood," Dad said. "Want to come along?"

The two of them left.

"My room was freezing this morning," I told Mom. "I could hardly get dressed."

"I know," she said. "It's so cold upstairs that I'm worried about Amy."

"Does Dad really know anything about furnaces?"

"I don't think so. But he hates to admit it. He's stubborn, just like his father."

This probably sounds stupid, but it's the first time I've ever heard anything about Dad's family. "Dad had a father?" I asked. "I mean, you knew him?"

Mom nodded. "Your father and I grew up in the same town. Later on, he got upset when his parents wouldn't pay for art school. He told them he didn't need them, that he'd earn the money himself. And he did. I think they wanted him to become an architect."

"But being an artist was Dad's dream!" I said. "I've always known that."

Mom spoke slowly. "I guess back then I was the only one who really understood that."

"What happened to Dad's family?"

44

"They moved away," Mom said. "I wasn't really involved at that point. We've never been in touch. I'm not sure they even knew your father and I got married!"

"How sad!"

"I know," Mom said. "It is sad. But your father's stubborn. He's a proud man!"

"But he always seems so happy-go-lucky!"

"He is happy-go-lucky now!" Mom said. "He's always said that what happened years ago wasn't going to ruin his life!"

"Will you tell me about your family?"

"Not tonight."

"I was just thinking," I told her. "It's so hard to think of you and Dad as *people!*"

"I know," she said. "Just like it's hard for me to think of Jason with a girlfriend!"

"I can't believe it! A little while ago, I was thinking the same thing!"

"I guess we never really grow older," Mom said. "We carry along with us the people we used to be. How about you, Katie? Can you think of yourself with a boyfriend?"

I shook my head and grinned. "Not really."

"Just wait." Mom smiled at me. "Would you believe I once felt the very same way!"

A New Look at My Family

Our family room, once warmed by the fire, was now warmed by close feelings. Although Mom and I had stopped talking, she now seemed like a special friend.

But when Dad and Jason came back in, the spell was broken. They were laughing and punching each other like they've always done.

Watching them, I felt confused. There was Jason, looking the same as ever. But he *wasn't* the same as ever! His world was no longer confined to this room. He has a girlfriend!

And there was Dad, looking the same as ever. But he wasn't the same either! He was proud and stubborn! And once he must have been terribly angry!

I looked at Mom. Mom, the good sport. Mom, who was always ready for adventure. Mom, whose laugh is so contagious that everyone else has no choice but to join in. Mom, the positive one, the loyal one, the *rock* in our family! I started wondering. Do I really know her?

"I'm going to start getting ready for bed," I announced. But nobody seemed to notice.

"OK, Katie," Mom said.

"Jason," Dad said, "we'll need to figure out a way to get more logs."

"Goodnight, everybody!" I said.

"See you tomorrow, Valentine!" Dad grinned at me. "Don't forget, tomorrow's Saturday. Jason and I will be making pancakes for breakfast!"

"And then we're off to see Mayblossom McDuff at the cabin," Mom said.

"I'll be ready," I promised. But nobody except my stupid dog even looked up. And January closed his eyes before I turned to go!

It was really hard to leave the fire and climb the stairs to my room. Not only is my room cold, it is still very ugly! My parents promised to paint it, but they haven't done it yet. I felt depressed.

The first thing I saw was my dolls. I've always had a good imagination, which is one reason I've enjoyed my dolls much longer than most kids. Audrey, B. B., and Gomer have been my faithful companions. And, frankly, in some ways they're better than either Jason or Sara Wilcox!

"Hi, Audrey," I said to my Cabbage Patch doll. But for the very first time, she didn't reply.

"Hi, Bronco Bob!" But the Denver Bronco souvenir didn't say anything either.

I picked up the lamb. "What have you got to say, Gomer?" He just smiled his weak little smile.

"I hate growing up!" I announced.

Nobody said a word.

I got undressed, but I nearly froze because I couldn't find my pajama bottoms! I got so cold I had to curl up in a little ball under the covers. I needed to get warm before I could go into the bathroom to brush my teeth.

"Even my dolls have deserted me!" I complained.

"I will never leave you or forsake you." That's what popped into my mind. It's in the Bible. The Lord said it.

"Lord, You really are here!" I said. "I know it!"

I relaxed. Suddenly, I wasn't as cold.

"I guess You know everything, Lord," I prayed. "But I don't. And, frankly, sometimes it's upsetting!"

I waited.

"First of all, there's my brother. For weeks now, I've been asking You to send Jason a

48

friend. But have You done it? No, You haven't!"

I paused.

"Yes, I know You provided a friend for me! Now, to be honest, Sara Wilcox wasn't exactly what I had in mind. But I'll have to admit that she's certainly making my life interesting! And now I finally have somebody to tell about You! Are You pleased?"

I could feel a smile beginning on my face.

Suddenly, I had a thought! Wow! What if Jason's friend wasn't what I had in mind either!

"You've got to be kidding, Lord!" I said. "Don't tell me You provided a *girl!*"

I started to giggle.

"I can't believe it!"

I giggled some more.

"Well, what do you know!"

I waited until I calmed down.

"OK, Lord. I'll give You that one! But then there's my father. And this one isn't so easy!"

I tried to put how I felt into words. "As You know, all my life, Dad's always been there for me!" I prayed. "Why, Lord, he's the one who always trusts You for everything! And You never let him down! Frankly, I've learned more about trusting You by living with Dad than I have from my Sunday-school teachers!"

I was almost arguing.

"Dad's such a kind man! And he's so funny!

And he loves us so much! I mean, I've always thought I have the perfect father!"

But even as I said it, I could hear Mom's voice. "Your father's a proud man." And I knew from the way she said it that it wasn't a compliment!

"He *is* a perfect father!" I said out loud.

But then, in my mind, I heard the voice of my Sunday-school teacher. "Nobody is perfect! Only Jesus is perfect!"

And I know she's right. That's what the Bible teaches.

"OK, so Dad isn't perfect!" I prayed. "He's still a wonderful father! And I'm lucky to have him. Right?"

Maybe things weren't as bad as I thought.

I waited. Then I started thinking about my mother. "Mom never complains. And she adores Dad!" Suddenly, I realized what I was saying. "But that can't be true! Lord, You're the One she worships!"

This was getting harder.

"OK, Lord, so Mom doesn't adore Dad," I prayed. "Let's just say she loves him a lot! In fact, she loves Dad so much that she's even given up her family in order to spend her life with him. She's incredibly loyal!"

What I said was true. I realized I was now warm enough to stick my head out from under the covers.

"But if she's really that loyal, how come she told me Dad isn't perfect?"

I waited.

And then it came to me. "Mom knew all along Dad wasn't perfect," I realized. "And she loves him anyway!"

I started to smile.

"I'm getting it, Lord! I'm getting it!"

I laid back on my pillow and relaxed.

Then I thought of something else. "That's exactly how You love me, isn't it, Lord?" I felt wonderful. "I mean, You know I'm not perfect, but You still love me! Right?"

And, although I didn't actually hear an answer, I knew in my heart it is true.

I opened my eyes. I discovered I wasn't depressed anymore. I got out of bed. Then I reached over, picked up Audrey, and tossed her up in the air!

"Watch it!" yelled Bronco Bob.

I got so tickled I nearly forgot to brush my teeth!

Silent Sam's Solution

When I woke up, my room was as cold as yesterday, maybe even colder. Again I hurried to get dressed and rushed down to the kitchen. My father was standing by the stove.

"You found your apron!" I said. Dad has this red and white striped apron he wears when he cooks. Because he's so large, Mom had to make it with extra long ties.

Dad turned and grinned. "It was packed with the linens in a box in the bedroom!"

Although Jason always helps Dad on Saturday morning, he wouldn't be caught dead wearing an apron! He likes to cook, but I happen to know that he thinks aprons are strictly for women. Now he was laughing. "Dad thinks wearing his apron will make the pancakes taste better!"

"It will!" Dad said. "You'll see!"

It was fun to see them so happy. I sat down at my place and waited. "Where's Mom?"

"She's dressing Amy," Dad said. "They'll be right down."

"Have you heard the joke about the farmer and the insurance salesman?" Jason asked.

Dad started to laugh. "You mean the one about the wagon wheel?"

Jason laughed too. "Who told you?"

They didn't notice when Mom marched into the room. She stood near the doorway holding Amy. "I hate to spoil your fun," she said. "But I'm really getting upset!"

"What's wrong, Elizabeth?" Dad asked.

"You know very well what's wrong, Steve!" she said. "Stop acting as if we don't have a problem! What are we going to do about this cold house?"

"Aw, Elizabeth," Dad said, "can't it wait? I'm all ready to pour the first pancake."

Mom put Amy into the playpen. "The baby's nose is running. Are you going to call somebody, Steve, or should I?"

"Take it easy, Mom," Jason said.

"You stay out of this, Jason!"

"I can't see anything wrong with the furnace," Dad said. "It looks OK to me."

"Then how come I'm freezing to death?"

"I don't know," Dad admitted. "To be honest, I don't really know what else to do!"

"I kind of gathered that," Mom said. "But there must be someone in town who understands old heating systems."

"Well, I guess we could ask Sam Johnson," Dad said. "You know, that curly-headed fellow in our Sunday-school class. Harry said he's a great handyman. How about if I call Sam when we get back from the cabin?"

Mom relaxed a little. "That's a good idea, Steve. But please call him before we go. I'll feel a lot better once I know this is being taken care of."

"Right," Dad said. "And now I'm going to make the first two pancakes. Is anybody still interested?"

"I'd like one," I said.

"Me too. I'm starved!" Mom said. And then she winked at me.

I smiled too. It was over as fast as it started. That's the good thing about Mom and Dad. Naturally, they don't always agree. But once something is handled, my parents don't stay mad.

Whether it was because of Dad's apron or not, I can't say. But the pancakes never tasted better!

"I feel sorry for people who have to eat pancakes in a restaurant!" Mom said. She says the same thing every week.

Before Dad could make his call, the telephone rang. It was for Jason. We watched as his face turned red. "I'll call you when we get home," he said. This time none of us said a word.

When he hung up, Dad glanced at Mom and went right to the phone. Unfortunately, the only time Sam Johnson could come was right away. Later on, he was driving down to Colorado Springs.

"I knew it," Jason said as we stacked the dishes. "Something always turns up to make us late. I wonder if this family will ever be able to get anywhere on time!"

"It won't matter today," I told him. "I'm sure M. McDuff won't mind. And this isn't like church. It can't start without us!"

"I know that," my brother said. "But I happen to have plans later on."

"With Allie?"

He nodded. "As a matter of fact, we're going to collect signatures on a petition. We want people to stop polluting our mountain streams."

"Oh," I said.

Sam Johnson turned out to be a neat guy. His curly hair is pure white. Sam doesn't just walk. Although he's much shorter than Dad, he takes gigantic steps. The funniest thing is that he doesn't talk. I mean, he hardly says a word! Unless you call *hmmmmm* talking. Personally, I don't. I gave him a nickname—Silent Sam.

"Actually, the furnace seems to be running all right," Dad told Sam.

He said, "Hmmmmmm."

"I thought we might be out of oil, but the gauge registers half full."

Silent Sam said, "Hmmmmm."

With Dad leading the way, the two men headed down to the basement. Before long, they were back.

"Hmmmmm," Sam said. This time he nodded when he said it. I watched as he kind of bounded into the dining room. Stopping at the fireplace, he looked up the chimney. "Here's your culprit," he said. "Hmmmmm. You happen to have another one?"

I couldn't believe it! Actually, when we first started fixing up Home Sweet Home, we had no fireplace at all. But eventually, we discovered two of them hidden behind walls. The fireplaces were Mom's pride and joy. She thought the Lord gave them to us.

I watched now as Sam shook his head. "Feel that draft?" he asked.

Dad nodded. "I guess we didn't notice it before because it was warmer."

Sam didn't waste time or motion. He leaped

over and put his hand next to the windows. "Feel this?"

Dad felt.

"A regular gale," Sam said.

Dad led the way, and Sam sailed through the hall into the family room. Next to the fireplace, Sam shook his head again. "Hmmmmm! What did I tell you!"

I waited while Sam followed Dad upstairs, two steps at a time. In no time they were back down.

"Want a cup of coffee, Sam?" Mom offered.

He nodded.

"You take something in it?"

Sam shook his head.

The whole family stood around and waited for him to speak.

"A regular sieve," Sam said. "That's the trouble with these big old wrecks!"

"What can we do?" Dad said. "I could put in a little weather-stripping. But we certainly can't afford storm windows and insulation."

"I suppose we could board up the fireplaces again," Mom said sadly.

"You got two choices," Sam said.

"Move out?" Jason asked.

"Not funny, Son!" Sam shook his head. "Two choices. You can bundle up in down jackets. But then you'll still go broke buying fuel oil."

He looked around at our solemn faces. Then

he broke into a big smile. "Or you can put in a wood stove. Think that's what I'd do!"

"Sam, could you help me?" Dad asked.

He nodded. "What kind?"

"We don't know anything about wood stoves," Mom said. "Couldn't you just recommend one?"

"I reckon," Sam said. He stood up and took off into the dining room. Stopping by that fireplace, he looked, poked, and measured. "This here's our spot."

"Whatever you say," Dad told him.

"Will you get the permit?"

"If you could take care of it, we'd be grateful," Dad said. "But Jason can help me. Right, Son?"

My brother nodded.

In a short time, it was all arranged.

After Silent Sam left, Mom hugged Dad. "You know, Steve, I have an idea," she said. "Actually, we're just rattling around here anyway! We could close off some of the rooms, and move the furniture around a little." She smiled. "Wouldn't the dining room make a wonderful winter living room! I mean, it's right next to the kitchen and everything!"

Dad smiled at her. "You're great, Elizabeth! I can't believe you're such a good sport!"

"But can we afford to buy a wood stove?" Jason asked. "How much is it going to cost?"

"It looks like we have no choice, Jason," Dad

said. "We certainly can't freeze to death!"

"Maybe the Lord wants us to sell the painting," I said slowly.

Dad smiled. "Maybe," he said. "And maybe not! This could be a test. Let's just wait and see what He tells us to do."

"Your father has so much faith!" Mom said. "In all the years we've been married, he's never doubted that the Lord would provide for us."

Dad smiled. "And He's always done it!"

"Well, maybe this time He provided the painting," Jason said. "Did you think of that?"

"He'll let us know," Dad said.

My brother turned away. "Hey," he said, "look at the time! Let's get started!"

We Return
to "Our" Cabin

By the time we finally hit the road, Jason wasn't the only one who wondered if we'd ever get to the cabin in Divide.

In addition to our delay with Silent Sam, we had trouble fitting everything and everybody into Purple Jeep. With Amy and her car seat, it's a tight squeeze! And January was nearly the last straw!

"I think we'll just have to leave the dog at home," Dad said.

"No, we can't leave January!" I protested. "The cabin was his home, too!"

"Maybe we should leave him anyway," Jason said. "Remember how he howls whenever he sees M.? Katie, don't you get embarrassed?"

My brother had a good point. Even I had forgotten. Last summer, every time January caught sight of Mayblossom McDuff, he sounded just like he was singing the "Star Spangled Banner"!

In my mind, I could still hear that crazy animal howl! *AaaaaOooooooo!* But I didn't want to admit it. "I think January's forgotten all about howling," I said. "Actually, he used to do the same thing whenever he saw Sara Wilcox. But he hasn't howled at her in weeks!"

January got to go. But when we finally got crammed into the car and headed north, Mom sighed. "I'm beginning to understand why families get station wagons!"

"All right!" I said. "Can we get one?"

Mom didn't answer.

Jason poked me and leaned over so she couldn't hear. "Even if the Lord would send us a station wagon, we'd probably just have to give it away!"

"Stop it, Jason!" I said. "Just because you're selfish doesn't mean the rest of us are!"

"I resent that!" my brother said. "I am not selfish! I'm just practical! Somebody in this family has to be!"

"Be quiet back there!" Dad yelled. Some things never change.

I turned and looked out the window. This was

familiar territory. I tried to figure out how many times I've traveled up and down Ute Pass!

Mom and Dad weren't talking. I wondered if they were thinking about the cabin. After all, it had been their home almost from the time they were married. But they had only rented it. And last summer, when the owner put the cabin up for sale, they couldn't afford to buy it.

"At least the cabin's still there," Mom said. "I'm glad it wasn't torn down to build condos!"

"True. And the land hasn't been spoiled," Dad said. My father used to talk a lot about *the land*. But this was the first time I heard him say those words since we moved.

"Steve, I was wondering," Mom said. "Do you think we'd have time afterwards to drive on up to Cochrans' ranch? I'd love to see her and show off Amy!"

Jason came to life. "Count me in! If it wouldn't take too long, I'd like to check out the sheep! And I just remembered something. I never did get to see those new puppies!"

"And maybe Katie and I could stop at Flat Rock," Dad said. "Are you interested, Valentine?"

"Not very," I said. "To be honest, I'd much rather see my old room."

"We'll have to be polite, Katie," Mom said. "Maybe M. won't offer to let you see the loft."

As we neared the cabin, my heart sank. The mailbox I had visited daily most of my life was gone!

"Look!" Mom said. "Mayblossom has a new mailbox! Isn't it attractive! I think it's supposed to be a model of the cabin!"

Dad drove up the lane. The shed was still there. The pine trees were still there. The bird feeder was still there. The bench near the front door was still there.

"Look!" I said. "She's painted the front door blue!"

"I like it!" Mom said. "I wish I had thought of that!"

Suddenly, the blue door opened, and Mayblossom McDuff stepped out! Smiling from ear to ear, she waved both arms in the air. "Welcome!" she called.

Before we even opened a car door, January woke up. He took one look at M. and pointed his nose in the air. *AaaaaaOoooooooooo!*

"So much for that theory!" Jason said.

The next thing we heard was a high peal of laugher. "Oh, good!" M. called. "I was hoping you'd bring January!"

And then Amy started to cry! I mean, our baby almost never cries! But you'd never know it from the way she was acting now!

"Oh, my!" Mom said.

"Shall we just leave?" Dad asked.

"Just a nice, quiet little visit from the Hoopers!" Jason muttered.

"Hi, Mayblossom!" I called over all the racket. "Guess what? We're here!"

She laughed again. "So I see!" she called. "Come here, Katie!"

I turned to my family. "I don't know about the rest of you," I said, "but I'm going!"

When I opened the car door, I sucked in my breath as I watched January take off like a rocket! Fortunately, he ran the other direction, not toward the house. I shrugged my shoulders.

I climbed down and started running toward M. "I brought you something!" I called. "I made them myself!"

She stood there with her arms open wide, and I ran right into them. We were both laughing and hugging each other. We didn't say a word.

"Let me get a good look at you, Katie!" she said, finally. I noticed that her eyes were all glistening.

I tried to catch my breath. "I nearly dropped the cookies!" I said. "Oh, no, I told you! I guess I still can't keep a secret!"

We both started laughing again.

"It's just wonderful to see you again, Katie!" M. said. "You look just the same!"

"You do too!" I said. She looks a little like pictures of my grandmother. Today M. was wearing nearly the same outfit she wore when I first met her up at Flat Rock—jeans and pink jogging shoes.

By now my family was coming up the path. Together, M. and I turned to watch them!

"Hi, M.!" Mom called. "We brought someone for you to meet! I'm sorry she's so noisy!"

M., still hanging on to my hand, walked toward Mom and Amy.

"She's certainly got good lungs!" M. laughed. "She's beautiful, Elizabeth! Just like the rest of you!"

"Even me?" Dad grinned.

M. laughed. "You even look good to me!" she said. "Life in town must be agreeing with you!"

"Hi, M.!" Jason said. "It's good to see you again!"

"Guess what?" I said. "He kind of has a girlfriend!"

"Jason! Say it isn't so!" M. laughed. "I was hoping *I* still had a chance!"

Jason smiled. "You do!" And he grabbed Mayblossom's free hand for a minute. I nearly fainted.

Meanwhile, all this time, Amy was still crying. "I guess I'd better feed her," Mom said. "It's the only way we'll get some peace and quiet."

"Let me hold her," I said.

Mom passed her over to me. The crying stopped!

"Katie, you have the magic touch!" M. said. She giggled. "That sounds like a good title for a book!"

And that's the first time today I even thought about the fact that M. McDuff is an author. She writes children's books.

As we passed through the new blue door, nobody spoke. The living room, with its big stone fireplace, certainly looked familiar. But it really wasn't our home anymore! I could see that right away.

Mayblossom McDuff didn't say a word. She stood off to one side, watching our faces.

After a few moments, Mom walked over and hugged her. "It's beautiful!" she said, and you could tell she really meant it. "It's perfect! M., this is really *you!*"

M.'s face broke into a huge smile. "I'm so relieved! I was hoping you'd like what I've done. And that you wouldn't feel too bad!"

"It looks a lot different with your furniture," Jason said. "But I like it too!"

"I expected to feel bad," Dad admitted. "But the funny thing is that I don't! M., I think this cabin was meant for you!"

M. got a funny look on her face. "That's just what I said to my friends in the East! When I first told them I was moving, they couldn't believe it! After all those years of talking about it, I actually bought a place in Colorado! But I expect they'll all be flying out to see me next summer!"

"Is this your same furniture?" Mom asked.

M. nodded. "My old house was much bigger, so I had to sell or give away a lot of things," M. said. "Would you like to see the rest of the cabin?"

"Oh, M.," I said, "I was really hoping I could see my room!"

Mayblossom smiled at me. "In a little while, Katie. First let me get you all a cold drink!"

Mom came over and took Amy. "This might be a good time to feed the baby. May I feed her in your bedroom?"

"Of course!" M. smiled. "I think you know the way!" Then she grinned right at me. "Now, Katie, how about helping me serve your cookies?"

I grinned back and followed her into the kitchen. I think that's when I realized something for the very first time. Sure, I know she likes Amy and the rest of my family. But to Mayblossom McDuff, I'm really someone special!

A New Relationship

"You and your friend certainly bake wonderful cookies!" M. said. "You could start a business!"

"No kidding!" I said. "Actually, we were thinking about it."

Jason grinned. "Unfortunately, the idea is like a donut! It has a few holes in it!"

Everybody laughed. But not very hard. I think they were just being polite.

"Well, M. McDuff, are you working on a book right now?" Dad asked.

"I've taken some time off to move and get settled," she said. "But I'll have to get started again soon. I have a deadline coming up."

"I never had the chance to thank you for telling your publisher about me," Dad told her. "Actually, I'm still surprised that they like my sketches so much. I've always thought of myself as a painter."

"Don't thank me," M. said. "It was strange the way it happened. I was so proud of my new home that I showed your sketch of the cabin to everybody who was willing to look! Actually, it was my editor who showed it to the art director!"

"Then it really was an answer to prayer!" I said.

M. looked surprised. "What did you say, Katie?"

With everybody looking at me, I felt kind of embarrassed. "That's how the Lord answered our prayer," I explained. "We need money because of the baby and everything. And the Lord showed us He didn't want us to manage a ranch!" I grinned. "I bet the Lord knew Dad doesn't like horses!"

Dad laughed. "Did you understand all that? Katie's stories can get pretty long and confusing!"

"I was trying my best to cut it short!" I said.

"Thanks!" Jason rolled his eyes. "We could have been here all day!" Then he looked at his watch. "Which reminds me. Dad, don't you think we'd better get going?"

"Just a minute," Mom said. "I want to ask M. about something. Is there a reason you seemed surprised when Katie mentioned praying?"

"Actually, I wasn't *too* surprised!" M. smiled. "I've wondered for some time if you were Christians. Am I right?"

I couldn't believe it. "How did you know?" I asked.

"You gave me lots of clues!" she said. She smiled even wider. "You see, I'm a Christian, too!"

"That's wonderful!" Mom said.

"Well, what do you know!" I said. "It's a miracle!" I ran over and hugged her.

"That's great news!" Jason said.

"We've just started going to an excellent church in Woodland Park," Dad said. "I think you'd find it worth the drive down every week."

"Harry Upjohn at the bank told me about a church there," she said.

"It's the same one!" I told her. "Now we go there, too!"

"I'll certainly think about it," M. said.

Again Jason looked at his watch. "Dad, if we're going to the sheep ranch, we really need to get started!"

"We'd love to stay longer, M.," Dad said. "But as long as we're this close, we want to stop to see the Cochrans."

"Of course," Mayblossom said.

"Can I stay here?" I asked. "M. and I have so

much to talk about. And I didn't get to spend nearly enough time in my room!"

"Katie's right! We do have a lot to talk about," Mayblossom said. "Please let her stay!"

"Are you sure she won't keep you from doing something?" Mom asked.

"I'm positive," M. said.

The first thing M. and I did after my family left was head for the loft.

"Dad hadn't been in the loft in years," I said. "I couldn't believe it when he started up this ladder!"

"To be honest, I was praying it would hold him!" M. laughed.

"Really? Me too!" I said. "My father's a big man, isn't he?"

Now I just stood in the doorway to my old room and looked in. "It sure looks different! Is this really where you write your books?"

"Well, I haven't written any in here so far," M. said. "But this is where I'll do it!"

I walked in and took a closer look at the book covers framed and hung on the wall. "Did you really write all these books?"

"Actually, I did them one at a time," she laughed. "You know, Katie, your room is my favorite place in the cabin. It's so cozy! I got the idea for putting the covers on the wall by seeing those sketches you had put up in here."

"You mean my birthday pictures," I said. "Dad sketches me every year on my birthday."

"Have you put them up in your new room?"

I shook my head. "We haven't had time to fix up my room. We've been very busy."

"I'm sure you have."

I looked across the hall. "Is Jason's old room really where your guests will sleep?"

M. nodded.

"He always kept it neat," I said. I decided not to tell her that no matter how I try, my own room's always a disaster.

"You haven't really given up this room, have you?" M. asked. "Does it still seem like it should be yours?"

I was surprised she understood. "Sort of," I said. "I guess I don't exactly feel at home in my new room."

"You can come up again if you want to, Katie," she said. "But wouldn't it be fun to fix a sandwich and eat it on the bench?"

I couldn't believe it. "That's where Mom and I used to sit," I said.

In spite of the season, the sun was warm on my face. Although the bench was hard, I didn't mind one bit. I ate slowly. "At my house, we never have tuna sandwiches."

M. grinned. "Now, Katie, tell me everything!"

"Everything?"

"What's been happening in your life since you moved from here?"

"I have to warn you," I said. "My stories tend to get pretty long! Frankly, whenever I try to tell anything, my parents get impatient! And Jason rolls his eyes!"

M. laughed. "I promise I won't get impatient or roll my eyes!"

And she didn't! I told her how we found Home Sweet Home and all about the treasure and the ghost. And, of course, that reminded me of my friendship with Sara Wilcox. I even told her about the awards I won in school.

"That's everything?" She grinned.

I was embarrassed. "You guessed!"

"What do you mean?"

"It wasn't really *everything!*" I explained. "Actually, I didn't tell you about the C I got on my term paper. Or how I keep losing January. To be honest, I just told you the good stuff!"

She laughed really hard! "That's wonderful, Katie!" she said. "There are too many people in the world ready to put us down! We all need someone to listen to the good stuff!"

"Mom and I used to talk more," I remembered. "Sometimes we'd sit here and talk for hours."

"She's been busy, with moving and the baby."

"I guess," I said. "Partly, it's just me. For some reason, now I don't want to tell her everything."

"Maybe it's because you aren't a child anymore," M. said.

I thought about that. She could be right.

"Katie, I was wondering. Do you have a grandmother?"

I shook my head. "Not exactly," I said. "One of them disappeared even before my parents got married. And there's something mysterious going on about the other one!"

"I don't have grandchildren either," M. said. "That's been one of the hardest parts of not getting married."

"You never got married?"

She shook her head. "A long time ago, my boyfriend was killed in the war. And, to be honest, nobody else ever asked me!" She grinned.

"You don't seem too sad."

She laughed. "I'm not sad! Being a martyr doesn't suit me. To be honest, I can hardly remember good old Bob! And the Lord has given me a wonderful life! I love what I do, and I have lots of friends!"

"Still, you'd make a super grandmother!" I said.

She smiled. "Do you really think so?"

"Anybody'd be lucky to get you!"

"I'm not so sure!" she said. Then she began to giggle. "Actually, Katie, you and I are a lot alike. I think you only know the good stuff!"

75

Now we both laughed.

"It doesn't matter to me!" I said.

"Me either!"

Suddenly, I had an idea. "Is there a rule that grandmothers have to be related to their grandchildren?"

"I guess not!" She laughed. "Are you thinking what I'm thinking?"

"We could adopt each other!" I said. "Is it a deal?"

She hugged me. "It's a deal!" she said. And when we stopped hugging, I saw that her eyes had filled with tears.

A Special Invitation

"Here comes January!" I said. "Oh, no. He's being chased by a rabbit!"

"I can't believe it!" M. laughed. "What a funny dog!"

"You don't know the half of it!" I said. "I could spend all afternoon telling stories about January!"

Frankly, I think the stupid dog was embarrassed. I mean, wouldn't you be! Anyhow, this time January didn't even think about howling! Without even glancing at M., he slipped in beside me, put his head in my lap, and began to whine.

I felt kind of sorry for him. I patted him gently. "Good dog!" I didn't know what else to say.

"I don't know much about dogs," M. said. "Do you think January might be hungry?"

"He eats at night," I told her. "But he could be thirsty. OK if I get him some water?"

January drank every drop, but it didn't stop him from whining. It was pathetic!

"Given a choice, I almost prefer his 'Star Spangled Banner' routine!" I said, laughing.

M. laughed too. "Is that what you call it when he howls?"

I nodded. "That's what it sounds like!"

Suddenly January was quiet! He sat up straight and seemed to be listening.

"Here comes your family!" Mayblossom said.

"The dog must have heard the car," I realized. "Maybe he isn't so stupid after all! At least his ears are OK!"

As Purple Jeep approached, M. smiled at me. "This has been so much fun, Katie!"

"I hate to leave!"

"You'll have to come back again soon!" M.'s eyes sparkled. "I have an idea! Maybe sometime you can stay overnight. Would you like to try out the new guest room?"

"Really?" I said.

"Really," she said. "If it's all right with your mother."

"And guess what? If you come to our church, I can see you on Sundays!"

She smiled as she stood up. "I thought of that, too!"

When Purple Jeep stopped, Dad rolled his window down. "If you don't mind, M., we won't get out of the car. Amy finally went to sleep, and Jason wants to get home."

"I understand," M. said. "I'm so glad you came! Having friends visit makes the cabin seem more like my home!"

"Did you have fun, Katie?" Mom asked.

"The best!" I said. "M. says maybe I can sleep over sometime!"

"Let's go, Katie!" Jason said. "Dad thinks we're due for some snow!"

Holding my hand, M. walked with me to the car. "You have a very special daughter," she said. "Thanks for sharing her!" She gave my hand a squeeze. "Goodbye, Katie Hooper!"

"I love you, Mayblossom McDuff!" I whispered.

I climbed into the back seat and held the door while January jumped in. Then, as Dad turned on the motor, the dog looked out at M. Suddenly he started howling! *AaaaaaOooooo!* I couldn't believe it!

M. McDuff looked right back at January. She pulled herself up as straight as a soldier. And, without smiling, she raised her hand to her forehead in a smart salute!

Everybody started laughing. "What in the world?" Jason said.

"She's saluting!" I said. "Don't you get it? She's doing it because January's singing the 'Star Spangled Banner'!"

"All we need is the rocket's red glare!" Dad laughed.

"Thanks for everything, M.!" Mom called.

"At ease!" Dad called.

I just smiled and waved. I had already said it all! This had been one of the best days in my whole life!

"That's enough, January!" Dad said. He turned on the radio. "I'm going to try to get a weather report."

I looked over at Jason. "Were Cochrans home? Did you get to see the sheep?"

At first my brother didn't answer. "In some ways I really miss our old life," he said.

"Me too," I agreed. But even as I said it, I realized how much I have changed these past few months. I've changed a lot! To be honest, it is very hard for me even to remember my old life!

As for January, he was sound asleep before we even turned onto the highway. Some things never change!

"I hate this music!" Mom told Dad.

"Why is it you can never get a weather report when you need one?" Dad asked.

Actually, we really didn't need one. The sky had clouded over and snow was beginning to swirl around the windows.

"I feel uncomfortable on the road during a snowstorm," Mom said. "Do you think it will be a bad one?"

"Don't get excited," Dad said. "I'll pull off if I can't see."

"I sure hope M. will be OK alone there at the cabin," Jason told me. He always thinks of things like that.

"Why wouldn't she be?" I asked. "She seems pretty self-reliant!"

"Think about it, Katie!" he said. "She's from a city in the East. What preparation does she have for living all alone in the mountains of Colorado?"

"She's come here lots of times on vacations," I remembered.

"In the winter?"

"I don't know." I tried to think. "The Lord will take care of her!"

"Sure!" my brother said. "Are you saying that nothing bad ever happens to Christians?"

"Quit it!" I told him. "Mayblossom will be all right! I just know she will!"

Jason didn't reply. In fact, we both stopped talking. Finally, he smiled over at me. "Is her name really *Mayblossom?*" he asked. "Mayblossom McDuff! What a funny name!"

"It's her name, all right!" I said. "That's why she lets us call her M.!"

"I wonder how she ever got a name like that!" Jason said.

"That's easy," I said. "I asked her the first time we met. She was named after a tap dancing teacher!"

He grinned. "You like her, don't you?"

"I do like her a lot!" I said. "You know what? I just asked the Lord to take care of her."

"I'm glad," he said. "Actually, I did too."

Suddenly it stopped snowing so hard. We had reached the other side of the storm. That happens sometimes. One place in the mountains can get lots of snow, and another place can get none.

"The skiers will be happy," Dad told Mom. "It's supposed to be a good winter for skiing!"

"I hope Sara and I can save enough money," I said.

"For skis?" Jason asked.

I nodded.

"If you start now, you probably could save enough money by the time you're in high school," he said.

"Why do you always have to be so negative?"

"I'm not negative," he said. "I told you before. I call it being practical."

"I'd love to!" I said. "Can Sara come too? You know, my friend Sara Wilcox."

"That would be wonderful! Thanks a lot!"

I hung up. I was very excited. This is the first time I've been asked. "I have to call Sara," I said. "We're going to work in the church nursery tomorrow!"

"Can't it wait until I call Allie?" Jason asked.

"I guess so." Grinning, I handed the phone to my brother. "Just keep it short!"

After Jason dialed, he realized the whole family was still in the kitchen. "Hey, you guys! Please leave! Can't I ever have any privacy?"

Dad and Mom both smiled. "Come on, Katie!" Dad said.

But before we even got into the hall to take our coats off, we heard Jason cheering. "She waited for me!" he yelled. "I'm going!"

"I knew she would," I said to myself.

"When will you be home?" Mom called. But it was too late. Jason was already gone.

I was pretty sure Sara would be only too happy to help. She has trouble sitting still in church anyway. "You're probably used to it," she said after her first time. "But I'm too big for that kiddie story, and the other one is way over my head! And those songs! Give me a break!"

I just let Sara complain. I'm glad she's honest! Since she rides with us, she has to stay for church anyway. If she wants to go to Sunday school, she has no choice.

Frankly, the first thing I thought about when Mrs. Upjohn called was that I'm finally old enough! Not to brag, but she only asks kids who are mature.

"You know what this means, don't you?" Sara asked, when I called her.

"Sure. It means Mrs. Upjohn thinks we're mature."

"Well, maybe," Sara said. "But what else?"

"It means you get out of going to church."

"Well, maybe," Sara said. "But what else? Think now!"

I thought. "I give up!"

"Remember when we were talking about babysitting? Well, this will count as experience! It will look fabulous on our resume!"

* * * * * * * *

Even though I was the one who invited Sara to Sunday school, she and I aren't in the same class. Actually, we were together the first week. Our lesson included the story where Jesus walked on the water. Well, Sara asked so many questions that we never even got Him back into the boat!

And from then on, somebody decided Sara

would be better off with Mrs. Pearson. She has a smaller class. It's mostly for kids who haven't grown up in Sunday school and need to learn the "basics."

After class today, Sara and I met by the drinking fountain.

"I'm really up for this!" she said.

"You're just supposed to help," I told her. "You aren't really in charge."

"So how old are the little monsters?"

"Some are babies, and the rest are toddlers."

"I'm familiar with babies," Sara said. "But what exactly are toddlers?"

"They're babies that walk," I told her.

"I get it!" she said. "Let's go!"

The nurseries for the two groups are next to each other, separated by a bathroom. Sara and I looked in through the glass in the doors.

"Piece of cake!" Sara said.

"When we open the doors, you'll hear the noise," I said. "Then you'll change your tune!"

Mrs. Upjohn saw us and came to the door. "Be careful," she said. "Don't let anybody out!"

"It's like a jail!" Sara whispered.

"Be quiet!" I told her. "They don't want little kids running all over the church, do they?"

"I thought you said Jesus loves them!"

"He does! But I'm sure He wants them in here, too!"

Mrs. Upjohn had already met Sara Wilcox at my house. She smiled when she saw her. "I appreciate your coming to help, Sara!"

"My pleasure," Sara said. "These must be the toddlers."

"I see you have some experience, Sara!" Mrs. Upjohn said. "Why don't you help in here! And Katie, you'll be perfect next door! We need someone like you to handle the infants."

"Good! I'd like that!" I said. "My sister's in there. May I cut through the washroom?"

Surprisingly, I found the crib nursery quiet. A pretty woman greeted me. "Aren't you Amy's big sister?"

I glanced at the baby in the crib next to the window. "Do we look that much alike?"

The woman laughed. "I should introduce myself," she said. "I'm Mrs. Stone. Your sister and my son, David, are kind of twins! They were born the same day at Penrose Birth Center."

I remembered several months ago, when Jason and I were waiting for Amy's birth. While he watched TV, I had talked to a sober little girl. She had announced that her mom was getting a baby boy. Frankly, I never figured out how she could be so sure. "Mrs. Stone, do you happen to have a daughter about three years old?"

"She's in the next room. You've met Doris?" Mrs. Stone asked.

I smiled. "We met in the waiting room at the hospital. If I remember correctly, I think she wants to be an electrical engineer!"

"That's Doris!" The woman laughed. "She's never really been a child! And she repeats everything she hears!"

Mrs. Stone excused herself and went to the door to receive a screaming baby from his mother. "Here's Joseph's bottle," the woman said. "And there's a diaper in this bag!"

As soon as Joseph's mother left, all the other babies joined in the chorus! Well, maybe not all of them cried, but it sure sounded like it! I got the responsibility of feeding the newcomer. I patted him and sat down in the rocking chair. "Hush, li'l baby, don't you cry," I sang.

By the time I got Joseph settled in a crib, Mrs. Stone gave me another assignment. "Well, of course you're crying, little one," I said. "Nobody likes wet diapers! I'll have you comfortable in no time flat!" And I did.

"Katie, you're wonderful with the babies!" Mrs. Stone said.

"Thanks." I smiled. "I've watched how Mom does it. And Amy's giving me lots of practice!"

"Katie, do you think you could handle two children at once? I've hardly been able to get out since David was born. What would you think about babysitting David and Doris?"

"I think I could do it," I said. "I'm not sure, but I think Doris liked me."

"To be truthful, she's a real problem!" her mother said.

"Maybe she's jealous of the baby," I said.

"You could be right! Last week Doris fed David baby shampoo! He bubbled for an hour!"

I've never known time to go so fast! The hour was nearly over when I went into the bathroom to rinse out a diaper. I peeked into the next room. I couldn't believe my eyes!

Sara had the children marching around in a circle. At the front of the parade was a big girl who looked like Doris. And Sara was singing, "We'll have a hot time in the old town tonight!"

"Sara!" I said.

She looked up and smiled. "How am I doing?"

"Where's Mrs. Upjohn?"

"She'll be right back. She just had to go get something."

"She left you alone?"

"Just for a minute," Sara said. "She said Doris's mother is right next door if I need her."

When the children saw Sara talking to me, they stopped marching. Sure enough! It was the same girl from the hospital! Doris never smiled. After glancing at me, she turned and punched out the little boy next to her.

"Quit it, you little monster!" Sara yelled.

Doris took one look at Sara and stopped.

"That's more like it!" Sara said. "Now march!"

At that point, Mrs. Upjohn appeared in the doorway and smiled. "No problems, I see!"

"Piece of cake!" I said to Sara. Then I had to get back with the infants.

A Family Day Surprise

Before we went home, my family met in Fellowship Hall to look at the wall where Dad's painting might hang. *If* we decide to give it to the church, that is! At breakfast, my father said it is up to the whole family. Unless we all agree to give it, he will try to sell the painting.

"Well, what do you think?" Dad said.

"About what?" Sara asked. She was still so excited about her success in the church nursery that she was almost dancing up and down.

"Dad just finished a new mountain painting," I explained. "He thought it would look good in this room, above the fireplace."

Sara looked around. "You know what? I've never been in here before."

"To be honest, neither have I!" I said.

"I'm not surprised," Mom said. "Fellowship Hall hasn't been used much. The addition to the church was just completed this summer."

"It's kind of bare, isn't it?" Sara said.

My father laughed. "That's what everybody thinks. But most of us are too polite to say so!"

Mom looked unusually serious. "Don't tease!" she said. "The decorating committee wants Fellowship Hall to be special! We aren't going to fill it up with old leftovers! It's going to be nice enough for wedding receptions!"

"Having Dad's painting in here would sure help it look great right now!" I said. "You should see it, Sara! It's really beautiful! The light just shines on the snow!"

My brother stood over near the windows holding Amy. "Well, Jason, what are you thinking?" Dad asked.

"Lots of things," he said. "For starters, my baby sister's getting hungry!"

"We'll go home now," Dad said. "But what do you think about the painting?"

My brother smiled. "I'll have to admit that I'm amazed, Dad! I mean, if you started out to paint a picture that would be perfect for this room, you couldn't have done it better!"

Dad was pleased. "Well, we'll talk more about it later," he said.

When we reached Sara's house, she acted as if she hated to get out of the car. "Thanks for the ride! Katie, are you sure you can't play this afternoon?"

I smiled at her. "Sorry," I said. "Did you forget that we have Family Day every Sunday?"

"I remembered," Sara said as she opened the car door. "But it never hurts to ask!"

"Tell your mother 'hi,'" Mom called. Then she turned to me. "How did you girls do in the nursery?"

"Fine!" I laughed. "Sara actually organized the toddlers! And I think Mrs. Stone might ask me to babysit!"

"Really?" Mom said. "Did you know that she and I had our babies at the same time?"

As we reached the back porch, we heard the phone ringing. "I think that phone has eyes!" Dad laughed. "It can tell when we get home!"

Everybody just expected Jason to answer. "This is Jason Hooper. Oh, hi, Allie!" Then he got this stupid look on his face. "Me too!"

"Do you think Jason's falling in love?" I whispered.

Mom grinned. "Don't be silly!"

"I think I'll ask him!" Dad said.

"Don't Steve," Mom said. "You'll just embarrass him!"

"I wonder what she looks like!" Dad said.

Jason gave us a dirty look. "I'm sorry, Allie. It sounds good, but I have other plans."

"He's playing it cool!" I said.

"It's about time!" Dad laughed.

"He's never looked happier!" Mom said.

Personally, I thought he looked sick!

Jason hung up the telephone. "Can't a person have any privacy around here?" He didn't sound mad, though. And he was having a hard time trying to stop grinning.

"Who's in charge of Family Day?" I asked.

Everybody looked at me and smiled.

"It isn't my turn!" I said. "I just did it last week! Don't you remember the backgammon tournament?"

"We remember!" Dad said. "Actually, I'm in charge today. After lunch, I want everybody to put on old clothes."

Mom and Jason looked at each other. "Not just old clothes," she said. "Real old clothes!"

From the looks on their faces, I decided that my whole family was already in on the secret.

"Surprise! We're having another painting party!" Dad said. "Katie, we're going to paint your room!"

I started jumping up and down. "I can't believe it!" Then I put my arms around Dad and just stood there grinning. "Hey, Dad. Are you going to paint our noses again?"

said. "Christian fellowship is so important! I want a beautiful place for that to happen!"

"Jason?" Dad said.

"It's by far your most beautiful painting!" my brother said slowly. "And, as I said before, it's perfect in Fellowship Hall. But I still feel anxious about paying for the woodburning stove! I'm sorry, but I can't help it!"

"Katie?"

"I love that painting!" I said. "To be honest, I hate the idea of never seeing it again! If we give it to the church, we can enjoy it, too!"

Dad smiled. "A good point," he said. Then he took a deep breath. "I can't exactly explain why that painting's so special to me. As you know, we've never given any others away. But I can't stop thinking that I'd really like to give this one to the Lord! And somehow I have faith to believe that He will work things out for the stove."

"Then let's do it!" Jason said. "I prayed about it during church. I told the Lord that if I were the only one holding back, I'd try to trust Him, too!" My brother's face broke into a big smile.

Everybody cheered!

Now, nobody felt tired! And as we watched, the second coat of white paint did the trick. Suddenly, my room looked all fresh and pretty.

"I hear you want stenciling around the ceiling," Dad said.

"I want my symbol—red hearts!" I told him.

"We'll have to wait until the walls are really dry," Mom said. "But we can do it this week!"

"And can we hang my sketches up? You know, kind of like I had them in the cabin?"

"Katie, I'll even help you do it!" Jason said. I nearly fainted.

At bedtime, I was still so excited that I couldn't sleep. Finally, I turned my light back on. The walls were still fresh and white! I turned off the light again and lay there smiling. Then, absolutely positive I'd still be awake in the morning, I must have finally dozed off!

I Get a Special Phone Call

When I woke up, my room still looked cool. And, frankly, it still *felt* cold! I wonder if having a woodburning stove in the dining room will help me keep warm up here? Maybe Silent Sam can find a way.

"I'm so excited!" I told Mom at breakfast. "When do you think we can do the stenciling?"

"Possibly tomorrow," she said. "I may have time to cut the stencil today. But the walls must be very dry, and I'll have to pick up some red paint."

Today I beat Sara to the bus stop. But Calvin and Christopher were already there.

"Hi, Love of My Life!" Calvin said.

"Don't be a jerk," I told him.

"She'll be sorry!" Calvin told Christopher. "When I'm famous and my picture's on a Wheaties box, she'll be begging for an autograph!"

Sara arrived just in time to hear the part about being famous. Frankly, it's a subject that's of particular interest to her. "Why would they put your picture on a Wheaties box?" she asked.

"Because I'm going to win a gold medal!" Calvin said.

"In what?" I laughed. "When did they start giving medals for the loudest belch in the middle school?"

Calvin laughed. "You have to think ahead! I'm ready just in case!"

Christopher looked serious. "Calvin's going in for freestyle skiing!"

"What's that?" Sara asked. Frankly, I was glad she asked. That way, I didn't have to!

"I've always been accused of hot-dogging," Calvin admitted. "But now I'm going to learn how to do real tricks! You know, twists, and turns, and somersaults."

"But isn't that dangerous?" I asked.

"Be still my heart!" Calvin said. "Katie, you really do care!"

"Of course!" I said. "I'd hate it if you broke your neck or something!"

Calvin grinned. "Well, Christopher, it's a start.

Even sympathy is better than nothing!"

"I think he really likes you!" Sara said when we got on the bus.

"Calvin? Get real!"

"Katie, I'm curious," she said. "What did your family decide about your father's painting?"

"We're going to give it to the Lord."

"Oh. I thought you were going to hang it in the church."

"Same thing," I told her.

"You mean to say you're just *giving* it to them?" Sara's eyes got big. "Wouldn't a painting like that be worth a lot of money?"

"I guess so. Hey, Sara, I have a surprise to show you. Want to come over after school to see it?"

"I'm free! Why not?"

After school, when we got to my house, there was a big blue truck parked in front.

"Either you have company or your father bought a pickup," Sara said.

"It must belong to Silent Sam."

"Silent who?" Sara asked.

"His name is really Sam Johnson," I told her. "Our house is freezing cold. He's going to put in a woodburning stove."

"How come you call him 'Silent Sam'?"

"It's because he doesn't talk! That's why! All he says is 'hmmmmmm'!"

103

When we entered my house, things were in an uproar. Amy was crying. As Mom watched, Dad and Silent Sam were moving our big couch.

"Tip it up this way!" Silent Sam said.

"He talked!" Sara said. "I thought you told me he only says 'hmmmmmm'!"

Dad heard Sara and started to laugh. When he laughs, he always gets weak. He lost his grip on the couch and dropped it. It landed right on Silent Sam's foot.

We watched Silent Sam wince. "Oh, shucks!" he said.

"Wow!" Sara said. "I thought for sure he was going to swear!"

Now Dad and Sam were both laughing.

"Katie, maybe you and Sara had better go upstairs until they get this furniture switched around," Mom said.

"Ta da!" I flung open my door. "Well, Sara, what do you think?"

"Now that's what I call a real transformation!" she said. "I always knew you could pick up your things if you just tried!"

"The walls, Sara! We painted the walls!"

"I just noticed! No offense, but I always thought you had the yuckiest walls I'd ever seen in my life!"

"Does that mean you like it?"

Sara grinned. "I do. All you need now is a

bedspread! Katie, don't you have a bedspread?"

I shook my head. "I used to have one. But Jason and I were giving a play, and I turned it into a curtain."

"How come you did that?"

"We couldn't find a sheet!" I explained. "Besides, it was brown and orange. It wouldn't have gone with the stenciling."

"What stenciling?"

"I'm going to have a border of red hearts around the top of the walls," I said. "Here, let me show you in Amy's room!"

We stood in the doorway of the nursery. "Those aren't hearts!" Sara said.

"I know that!" I said. "Don't you think I know the difference between a teddy bear and a heart!"

"I was beginning to wonder," she giggled.

"Amy's symbol is a teddy bear, so Mom stenciled teddy bears in her room!" I told her. "My symbol happens to be a heart."

"I don't get it!"

"It's a tradition. Everybody in the Hooper family gets his own symbol," I explained. "Jason's symbol is a rainbow. My mother's is a lamb, and Dad's is a tree."

"What kind of a tree?"

"I don't know. Just a tree. I think it's in the Bible."

"No kidding!" Sara said. "Does your father have trees stenciled in his room?"

"Nope," I giggled. "But when he signs his paintings, he draws a tiny tree next to his name."

Sara looked at me. "I've noticed all the pillows and things in your house with lambs on them."

I smiled. "Mom loves lambs. People are always giving her things with lambs on them."

"I get it! Then that's why so many of your things have hearts on them!"

I nodded. "I thought you knew that."

Sara didn't say anything for a few minutes. "OK, now how can I get a symbol?"

"I don't know. You really aren't a Hooper," I said. "You're just a friend."

"I know that!" She put her hands on her hips. "But nobody can stop me from picking out a symbol for myself, can they?"

"I guess not. What symbol do you want?"

She thought a minute before her face broke into a big smile. "I've got it! I want to be a star! My symbol is going to be a star!"

"That's a good idea!" I said. "And you know what? Now we can write secret notes to each other. And nobody else will know who they're from!"

Later, as Sara was putting on her jacket, I thought of something. "Remember the other day? You were right. Jason's phone call was from a girl."

"I knew it!" she said. "What's her name?"

"Allie Meredith."

"She sounds beautiful!" Sara said. "Is she?"

"Is she what?"

"Beautiful?"

"I've never seen her!" I explained.

"Take it from me," Sara said, confidentially. "With a name like that, she's got to be beautiful!"

The phone began to ring. "Maybe it's her!" I said. "Wait a second, and I'll tell you exactly what she sounds like!"

As Sara watched, I spoke with my coolest voice. "Hello. This is Katie Hooper!"

"This is Mrs. Stone," said an excited voice. "I'm really stuck, Katie! Could you babysit for a couple of hours tonight?"

I couldn't believe it! My first job! I stood there grinning. "It just so happens that I don't even have any homework! I'll ask Mom and call you back!"

"It was Mrs. Stone!" I told Sara. "You won't believe this! She asked me to babysit!"

Sara answered in a quiet voice. "Just you?"

I nodded.

Sara never even smiled. She opened our back door. "See you tomorrow." That's all she said.

I Find a Career
(But Lose a Friend)

I wondered what Mom and Dad would say about my babysitting on a school night.

Actually, my parents were in an excellent mood. They were sitting and drinking coffee in what used to be our dining room. With the furniture all changed around, it looks very different. Now it has chairs and lamps, and it is cozy—like a living room.

"Hey, I like it! It looks great!" I said. "But what can we call it?"

"Let's call it our *keeping room*," Mom laughed. "Once the wood stove's installed in the fireplace, it will be *keeping* us warm all winter!"

As for the babysitting, my parents presented no obstacle at all! I think the fact that they know the Stones helped a lot. And I really didn't have homework.

"I'm going to save every penny I earn!" I told Jason. "In no time, I'll be skiing!"

"If you say so." I don't think he was paying any attention. He smiled. But frankly, now he smiles a lot more than he used to.

"Do you have any of your old toys around?" I asked him.

"Like what?"

"I don't know. Somehow I got the impression that Doris isn't really into dolls! I thought maybe she'd like a truck or something."

"You'll have to ask Mom," he said. "I think she saved some of my things."

But Mom can't remember what box she packed anything in! It's like she was in a trance during our entire move.

"I think I'll take Bronco Bob," I told her. "I think Doris might like him. Mom, am I dressed all right?"

She laughed. "You look fine, Katie! Don't forget! If you run into anything you can't handle, call me, and I'll come right over!"

"Mom!" I said.

"Well, you never know! It's not easy taking care of two children at once!"

I was all ready and waiting in the kitchen when somebody knocked at our front door. "I'll get it," I yelled, as I ran to answer it.

"Are you Mr. Stone?"

The man smiled. "I am. You must be Katie Hooper!"

"You know what? You're the first person who ever came to our front door," I told him.

He laughed. "Hi, Steve!" Dad had come into the hall, and now he was shaking Mr. Stone's hand. "We'll have her back in a couple of hours. Thanks for helping us out."

"No problem!" Dad said.

I felt left out of the conversation. But once Mr. Stone and I got into his car, I couldn't think of anything to say. I just sat there!

"I hear you have experience with babies," he said.

"I've been helping Mom take care of Amy," I told him.

"We've been using an older woman to sit for us," he said. "But you certainly made a good impression on my wife at church yesterday!"

"Thanks." I looked down. Bronco Bob laid there on my lap. He didn't say anything!

The Stones live in a house a lot like the one my family almost rented. I think it's called a bi-level. Right off the bat, you have to make a decision about going upstairs or downstairs! As we walked up the stairs, I noticed how warm the house was.

Mrs. Stone was waiting in the living room. "Hi!" she whispered. "We're in luck! They're both asleep!"

"That's nice," I said. I couldn't think of anything else.

"Follow me, and I'll show you around." She took off down a short hall. We peeked into the back bedroom and saw a sleeping baby in a crib. "If you need anything for David, you'll find it next to his changing table," she told me.

"Where's Doris?" I whispered.

"I'll show you." We headed off down the stairs. Without a word, Mrs. Stone opened a door. There, in a big bed, was Doris—sound asleep.

"She's out like a light!" Mrs. Stone said. "She didn't have a nap today."

Back upstairs in the kitchen, Mrs. Stone showed me the telephone. "Here's the number where we can be reached as well as the emergency numbers. And, if David wakes up, you can give him this bottle."

I nodded.

"You should be comfortable," she said. "My husband just put wood in the stove. Can you think of anything else?"

I couldn't. And in no time, I heard their car drive off.

I was all alone. Actually, I guess I never expected Doris and David to be asleep. Now I wasn't sure what I was supposed to do with myself.

I sat down on the living room couch. Naturally, the first thing I saw was the television. Since we've never had one, I really kind of wanted to turn it on. But, frankly, I was afraid it would blast so loud it would wake the children. Or, with my luck, maybe I'd break it! So I decided I'd better just leave it alone.

Of course, reading would have been perfect! How I wished I had brought a book! I reached over on the coffee table and picked up a magazine. It was about playing golf.

Figuring the Stones had to have books somewhere, I went downstairs to search. In the family room, I found a huge bookcase. Most of the books had hard bindings and looked like college textbooks. And the rest were children's books for Doris.

Disappointed, I turned and looked at the woodburning stove. It was black, and it sat on a tile platform. Although I couldn't see any fire, the room felt warm and cozy. As a matter of fact, compared to our house, it was hot! I slowly climbed the stairs.

As I sat down again in the living room, I looked at my watch. I couldn't believe it. Only ten minutes had gone by!

To be honest, this was absolutely the most boring two hours in my entire life! I was so desperate, I talked to Bronco Bob myself! The neatest thing I did all evening was peek in their refrigerator!

Was I ever glad to hear that car turn into the driveway!

"Hi, Katie!" Mrs. Stone said. "How did it go?"

"Fine," I said. "Just fine."

"I knew I could count on you!" she said. "I hope you can help us out again!"

I smiled. "I'd be glad to."

When Mr. Stone stopped the car in front of my house, he asked me how much I charge.

I decided to be honest. "I don't really know," I told him. "What was it worth?"

He laughed really hard. Then he handed me several bills. "Will that cover it?"

"I'm sure it will!" I said, grinning.

"We'll be calling you again, Katie!" he said. While I ran to the house, he waited in the car until Mom came to the door and waved.

"How did it go?" she asked.

"I think I found a career!" I told her.

The next morning I could hardly wait to tell Sara all about it. But when I got to the bus stop, Sara didn't say anything. "Aren't you going to ask me how the babysitting went?"

"I wasn't planning to," Sara said.

I decided to ignore her and tell her anyway.

"Both kids slept the whole time!"

"That was a lucky break!"

"Actually, it was boring," I told her. "Next time I'm going to take a book."

"You're going back?" she asked.

"If they ask me."

"How much did you get?"

I told her.

Her eyes got big. "It isn't fair!" she said. "The whole thing was my idea!"

"What do you mean?" I said. "Sara, you never invented babysitting!"

"I know exactly what's going to happen! You'll get skis, and I'll be left behind!"

"I can't help it! Sara, it isn't my fault if you don't have babysitting experience!"

"You didn't need experience!" she said. "The kids didn't even wake up!"

"They might have," I pointed out.

"As a matter of fact, I don't believe you really need the money anyhow," Sara said. "You aren't poor! You're rich!"

I couldn't believe my ears. "Are you kidding? Besides, how do you know?"

"Well, I'm not as dumb as I look!" she said. *"My* family isn't going around giving away expensive paintings!"

"You're just jealous because I earned a little money! What kind of friend is that?"

"No kind," Sara said. "And as far as I'm concerned, you can go find somebody else. That's what I'm going to do!"

At that point, the boys arrived at the bus stop. "Why is Sara standing over there by herself?" Calvin asked.

"Beats me!" I said. "Why don't you ask her!"

Sara Remembers Something

I've discovered that it isn't always easy being Sara's friend. But you don't stop liking someone because it isn't easy!

When the bus came, I sat in our usual place and waited for her.

"You still want to sit with me?" she asked.

"Of course," I said. "Why wouldn't I?"

"I acted pretty awful."

"I'm not perfect either!"

"You aren't?" We both giggled.

"Sara, there is something I'd like to explain." My voice was surprisingly calm. "We really *aren't* rich! That isn't why we're giving Dad's painting to the Lord!"

"Is it a bribe?" Her eyes got big.

"I don't know what you're talking about!"

"Well, if you give Him the painting, maybe the Lord will give you something back!" Sara said. "Something even better!"

"I guess that's possible," I said slowly. "But that isn't why we're doing it."

"I know!" she said. "It will make a great impression on the people at church! You'll get more popular!"

"You just don't understand, Sara," I said. "Sometimes people give things because of love! There doesn't have to be another reason!"

"You're right," she said. "I guess I don't understand."

I gave up trying to explain. It really didn't matter. At least Sara and I were still friends!

After school the blue truck was back at my house. "Silent Sam's at your house again," Sara noticed. "I hope he didn't think I was rude."

I shook my head. "He liked you. He said you're a Phyllis Diller! Whatever that means!"

"He said that? No kidding!" Sara seemed pleased. "You've heard of her, haven't you?"

I shook my head.

Sara grinned. "She's a very famous actress!"

We found Silent Sam on his knees in our keeping room. He was cementing tiles on the floor in front of the fireplace.

"How come you're doing that?" I asked.

He looked up. "Fire protection. Building code." Then he winked at Sara and said, "Hmmm-mmm!"

Sara and I both giggled.

On the way to my room, we found Mom in the nursery. "Hi, girls! Katie, Mrs. Stone called. She wants you to babysit Friday night."

I glanced at Sara. "That's nice," I said slowly.

"Is something wrong, Katie?" Mom asked.

"We both wanted to babysit," I told her. "But I'm the only one getting jobs!"

"I didn't realize you were so fond of children, Sara," Mom said.

"Frankly, it's more the money," Sara said. "Both of us decided to save up for skis. And now I'm left out. I don't know what to do."

"I see," Mom said. "When I have a problem I can't solve, I pray about it. Have you tried that?"

I nodded. "In the very beginning, we asked the Lord to help us get skis."

"No, we didn't," Sara said. "We just talked about praying. We never actually *did* it!"

I looked at her. She was right! "Come on, Sara! And thanks, Mom!"

"You're welcome!" she laughed. "Anytime!"

Sara and I went straight into my room and closed the door.

"I'm sorry, Lord," I prayed. "It was really all

my fault! Sara wanted to pray, and I put her off. And then I forgot all about it!"

"Here's the problem, Lord!" Sara prayed. "We need money for skis. You probably helped Katie get started babysitting! But how about me?"

"Yes, Lord," I interrupted. "I don't exactly see how she could help me at Stones'! So could you please get her a job of her own?"

"Thanks a lot, Lord!" Sara said.

I added an "Amen."

"That wasn't hard," she said. "I'm sure the Lord will come up with something!"

"Sure, He will!"

"Katie, I'm sorry I got ticked off this morning. Please forgive me!"

"Of course!"

I suppose I really should have kept my mouth shut. But, no! I had to go and explain to Sara what the Lord was going to do next!

"Here's how prayer works," I said. "First, He puts you in the church nursery so people will know about you! Now, I bet you'll get a call from one of the mothers!"

The next morning, Sara was waiting at the bus stop. "Nobody's called so far!"

"It's only Wednesday," I said.

"Just so He doesn't forget," Sara said.

"He can't forget!" I told her. "After all, He's God, isn't He?"

119

The next morning I could hardly wait to find out what happened. Actually, I didn't even have to ask.

"Nobody called me last night!"

"Don't worry!" I told her. "The Lord is probably teaching you patience."

"OK," she said.

Actually, Sara wasn't too uptight. To be honest, I was the one who was getting more and more nervous!

After school on Thursday, Sara came over to watch my mother stencil. Before Mom climbed on the stool, she let us try stenciling hearts onto some newspapers.

"Not so much paint, Sara!" Mom said. "The brush should be almost dry!"

Once Mom began, the stenciling along the ceiling went quickly. She'd tap paint into two sections of hearts. Then she'd jump down and move her stool, and stencil two more. The paint dried fast. Almost like magic, my walls had a border of red hearts around the top.

"Mom, it's wonderful!" I said. "My room is absolutely awesome!"

"I agree!" Sara said. "Now all you need is a bedspread!"

Mom smiled. "Actually, I have another idea! Katie, how would you like to make yourself a quilt?"

I saw right away what she had in mind. I grinned. "I could put hearts on it! Right?"

Mom's eyes twinkled. "You read my mind!"

"Mrs. Hooper, did you know that I have a symbol too?" Sara asked.

"I guess I didn't," Mom said. "Do I dare ask what it is?"

"It's a star!" Sara said proudly.

"That's what she wants to be," I explained.

"Sara, maybe you'd like to make a quilt, too," Mom said.

"Oh, could I!" Sara was thrilled. "How do you do it!"

"You can cut your symbols out of material printed with country designs," Mom said. "Then you can sew them onto white squares."

"I know!" I said. "And then we can sew all the squares together."

"Did you say *sew?*" Sara's eyes got big. "Just exactly how do you do that?"

"Oh, my," Mom said. Then she smiled. "It's all right, Sara. I'll help you learn! Everybody has to start somewhere!"

"How come you're so nice to me?" Sara asked.

"Why, Sara," Mom said, "we love you!"

"That's right!" I said.

By now I was really getting anxious about who would call Sara—and when! I never brought up the subjects of babysitting or skiing.

And, to be honest, I almost dreaded hearing Sara's daily morning reports.

"I waited all evening, but nobody called!" Sara told me.

I didn't know what to say.

"It's OK," Sara said. "Actually, I can hardly wait to see my favorite programs tonight! I'd sure hate to be babysitting and miss my favorite TV programs! And we haven't had any more snow anyway!"

"Right," I said, trying to smile. This was not going as I expected. Not at all!

Sara (And I)
Keep Waiting

Although I couldn't talk about it to Sara, I was pretty excited about babysitting at Stones' again. This time, they wanted me to come earlier and stay longer. It sounds kind of awful, but I figured I'd probably get more money!

After supper I put on jeans and laid out my jacket. I didn't even bother with a toy for Doris. Instead, I set out a brand new library book.

"All set, Katie?" Mr. Stone asked.

"All set!" I grinned.

But when we got out of the car I knew I was in trouble! From the front yard, I heard the baby crying. And as Mr. Stone opened the front door, his wife was yelling, "That's enough, Doris! You want Katie to like you, don't you?"

"No, I don't!" Doris replied.

Mr. Stone looked at me and shook his head. "Are you sure you can manage?"

I smiled bravely, "I'll do my best!"

Actually, things went much better after Mr. and Mrs. Stone left! I ended up reading to Doris while I fed David his bottle. Then it took me at least half an hour to get the baby settled down.

"Finally!" Doris said. "The kid's asleep!" To be honest, I felt the same way.

Doris watched me lay her brother in his crib. After she led me to a chair near the woodburning stove, she pulled out another book. "Now read this one!" she demanded.

"Doris, you really should say *please*," I told her. "When you say *please*, then I'll want to do it more!"

"OK," she said, *"please* read this book!"

I did.

"Now, *please* read this one!"

I did. Actually, before we finished, we went through the entire bottom shelf of the bookcase!

"Now, *please* play a game!" she said.

I was tired—and desperate. "No, thank you!" I told her.

"My mother promised you'd play with me!" she whined.

"What do you want to play?"

She got out *Chutes and Ladders*. Although I

hadn't played it in ages, it was always one of my favorites.

But Doris cheated! I don't know any other way to put it. Actually, I'm used to losing, but at least my brother plays fair!

Well, Doris did finally go to bed. But by then, I was too tired to even open my book. One thing was certain, I had really earned whatever money I would get this time!

When the Stones got home, they acted very impressed that the children were both asleep.

"I hope you didn't get cold, Katie!" Mr. Stone said. "I didn't realize the wood was low."

"Don't worry about it!" I said. "Our house is much colder! But we're getting a woodburning stove, too!"

"This one was here when we bought the house," Mrs. Stone said. "It saves us a lot of money."

Speaking of money, I did get even more than the first time! And Mrs. Stone wants me to sit every Friday night.

Frankly, I was sure the Lord would answer Sara's prayer by now! I couldn't believe she hadn't received a single babysitting call. There had to be a reason.

"Maybe it's because you weren't home," I told her Saturday afternoon. "You do spend a lot of time at my house."

"I'm home every night," Sara said. "How long do you think patience takes?"

"I don't know," I admitted. "Maybe you should pray again."

"I'll just wait," Sara said. "I'd hate to have Him think I'm bugging Him!"

To be honest, it was kind of embarrassing. I'm the one who's been a Christian since I was little. And now Sara's the one who still believes He's going to answer her prayer!

"Did Mrs. Upjohn call you?" I asked. "Are you going to work in the nursery again tomorrow?"

She nodded. "Are you?"

I smiled. "Uh huh. You know what? She told Mom you are very good with the toddlers."

"She did?"

"Sara, I have an idea. Maybe you could pin up a little sign with your name and telephone number on it."

"Sure," Sara laughed. "But if I'm going to advertise, I'd rather use the church bulletin board in the front lawn!"

I giggled.

"Katie, I don't think I have to do anything else," Sara said. "I just have to wait."

Well, it was easy for her to say. Personally, I felt that unless the Lord worked out a job for Sara soon, I'd be a basket case!

On Sunday morning, I got up early with something else on my mind. I took out a pencil and paper. Smiling to myself, I figured out how much money to put into the collection.

After setting aside the Lord's share, I looked at the money that was left. I've never had so much! And poor Sara has none! It just didn't seem fair.

"You could share it with her!"

I'm not sure where the thought came from. But I knew right away that it was a wonderful idea! After all, we did plan this skiing adventure together! And, to be honest, without Sara it probably wouldn't be half as much fun!

Frankly, I was so excited I could hardly wait! I put Sara's half of the babysitting money in an envelope in my purse. I'd give it to her after Sunday school!

Sara was waiting at the curb for Purple Jeep. "Did you do your Sunday-school lesson last night?" Sara asked me. "Did you learn the verse?"

I laughed. "It's pretty amazing that it turned up this week, isn't it!"

We said the memory verse out loud together: "Do not be anxious about anything, but in everything, by prayer and petition, with thanksgiving, present your requests to God. Philippians 4:6."

"That's wonderful, girls!" Dad said.

"Jesus doesn't forget prayer requests, does He?" Sara asked.

"Of course not!" Mom said.

"Sometimes His answers take a while," Jason said, with a big smile.

After Sunday school, Sara and I met before we went into the nursery. I gave her the envelope.

"What's this?" she asked.

"It's for you," I said. I couldn't stop smiling. "It's a start toward your skis!"

She looked inside. "What in the world, Katie! Is this your babysitting money? You don't have to do this!"

"I know I don't," I said. "I just want to."

"I can't believe it. It isn't Christmas! And it's not my birthday!" Sara said. "Except for those days, nobody's ever given me anything before!"

"The Lord has," I told her. "You probably just didn't realize it."

Sara looked me straight in the eye. "Katie, are you helping God answer my prayer?"

"I don't think so. That wasn't what I had in mind!"

"But why?" she asked. "Tell me why you're sharing your money like this."

"There's no reason," I said. "Only that you're my best friend, Sara, and I love you!"

"I don't know what to say," Sara said.

I grinned. "How about 'thank you'?"

She hugged me.

"Now, let's go take care of those children!" I said.

Compared to last Sunday, I had a very quiet day with the infants. I spent most of my time playing with my own sister! Not to brag or anything, but Amy's the cutest one in the nursery!

On the way home, Dad told us about a party to dedicate Fellowship Hall. "Would you like to come with us, Sara?"

"Are these the same people who had the party and brought all that great food when you moved to Woodland Park?" she asked.

"That's right!" Mom said. "You were there, weren't you!"

"When did you say that is?" Sara asked. "I'll put it on my calendar." She giggled.

"Next Saturday night," Dad said. "Jason, would you like to bring a friend, too?"

Jason smiled. "I just might!" he said.

Sara's Prayer
Is Answered

I guess I really didn't expect anybody to call Sunday and ask Sara to babysit. And I found out I was right. Nobody did.

"When you worked in the nursery yesterday, did you meet any of the mothers?" I asked her on Monday morning.

"Not even one," Sara said. "Mrs. Upjohn takes charge when the kids come and go."

"But surely the mothers must have seen you! I just know someone will call this week!"

On Tuesday, Sara was standing at the bus stop. "He still hasn't answered my prayer!" she told me.

"I can't stand it any longer!" I said. "Sara, how can you be so cool?"

"I don't know," she grinned. "I'm not usually like this!"

"Sara, I've been thinking about it," I said on Wednesday morning. "Maybe the Lord has a lot on His mind! Let's just remind Him you're still waiting!"

"Go ahead," Sara said. "Personally, I think I'll just wait to see what He does!"

Thursday morning was the same old story. I shook my head. "I can't believe nobody's called! It's almost the weekend again!"

"Tell me about it!" Sara said. "By the way, did Silent Sam finish putting in your woodburning stove?"

"It even works!" I told her. "When can you come over to see it?"

She smiled. "I don't have too much homework. Maybe I could come over later this afternoon."

When I got up Friday morning, I could hear the wind, and my room was freezing. I moved fast!

I met Jason as he was coming out of the bathroom. "Did you look out the window?" he asked. "I wonder if we'll have school?"

Back in my room, I pulled up my shade. The whole world was white! That's all I could see.

Dad was down in the keeping room muttering to himself as he tried to get the stove started. "It looked so easy when Sam did it!"

"Well, Katie, is this enough snow to get you excited?" Mom asked.

"How deep is it? I couldn't tell from my window."

Dad overheard us. "It's a big storm, all right! The snow nearly covered my boots where it's drifted! And it's still coming down!"

Jason rushed into the kitchen. "How come nobody put the radio on? I bet you anything the schools are closed!"

As you probably know, whenever you're waiting for something to come on the radio, it seems like it never does. And then, just as you start to talk, you miss the announcement! Which is why Jason was the only one who actually heard the news.

"No school!" he yelled.

"No kidding!" I yelled. I started jumping up and down.

"Let's celebrate!" Mom said. "This calls for something besides oatmeal! Steve, would you like to make pancakes?"

"I might as well," Dad said. "I'm sure not having any luck with this stove!"

"Don't let it ruin your life," Mom said. "It's no big deal. We can ask Sam to come back and give us another demonstration."

"I'll figure it out myself!" Dad told her. "Just give me time!"

"I can't believe it!" Mom said. "Here we go again!"

In spite of problems with the stove, breakfast was almost like a holiday! Once Dad put on his big apron, he forgot to be stubborn.

"Can Amy have a bite of pancake?" I asked. "She's smiling. She looks like she wants one!"

"It won't be long," Mom said.

I guess January felt left out. He sat near the kitchen door and whined.

"He hasn't been out yet," Mom said. "I was afraid he'd get lost."

"I'll take him," I offered.

"Don't *you* get lost!" Mom laughed.

I thought she was just being motherly until I opened the door! Wind whipped the snow into my face. Frankly, I couldn't even see January! I never had a chance to leave the porch. In no time flat, the dog was back begging to go inside!

"What's it like now?" Dad asked.

"I think it must be getting worse," I said. "It's a regular blizzard!"

There's nothing my mother loves more than an adventure! "We're practically snowed in!" she said. "Isn't this cozy! Now if we still had a working fireplace, we could curl up by the fire and read!"

"We can read anyway," Dad pointed out. "And don't blame me for the fireplace. You were the one who wanted it warm in here!"

By afternoon, the storm had passed. But not before it had dumped a thick blanket of snow all over Woodland Park.

Purple Jeep was totally buried. The snow was so deep that I nearly broke my back helping Jason and Dad shovel. Even as we worked, a plow made a pass down the road and piled up more snow. We finally finished.

"I'm going to Sara's," I said. "OK?"

When I got to her house, I was surprised. The Wilcox driveway was clear! Since Sara and her mother live alone, I wondered who had helped them out.

I walked up the path to the front door and pushed the bell. Nothing happened. I pushed it again.

"Ka-tie! Ka-tie Hoop-er!" yelled Sara's voice. It was mingled with the sound of a motor. I looked around.

"Over here!" she yelled.

I turned. There was Sara, her red hair sticking out of a wool cap. She was hanging on behind a huge snow blower! A gigantic arc of snow shot off to her left!

"Kat-ie! Come o-ver!" she yelled.

When I reached her, she leaned down and turned something. The noise stopped.

A smile covered Sara's face. "It's my answer!"

"What are you talking about?"

"The snow blower!" she said. "This is how the Lord answered my prayer!" She was so excited she could hardly talk.

"Take it easy," I said.

"I can't! I've already made more than your entire babysitting money! Katie, I'll give your money back! I don't need it anymore! At this rate, we'll both have skis in no time!"

"That's wonderful!" I said. "How come you didn't think of this yourself?"

"We didn't have a snow blower back in Omaha," Sara explained. "When we were moving, a friend of Mom's loaded this one on our van. He thought we might need it here!"

"Is it hard to use?" I asked.

"Mom thinks so," Sara said. "When it comes to anything mechanical, she's totally useless! But after she left, I figured it out!"

"How'd you get the jobs?"

"It was a cinch, Katie! People saw me doing my own snow and asked me to do theirs! I didn't even have to advertise!"

I had to laugh. "And I was so sure the Lord was going to have someone from church ask you to babysit!"

Sara giggled. "I got faked out, too! I really never expected Him to do anything as spectacular as this snowstorm!"

Well, I guess I'll never learn. "Actually," I explained, "the Lord probably thought you need more experience before He got you babysitting jobs!"

"Could be!" Sara grinned. "On the other hand, maybe He just didn't want me to miss my favorite television programs! Will we ever know for sure?"

We Dedicate
Dad's Painting

By Saturday night, the snow had just about disappeared. Sara says snow lasts longer in Omaha, but sometimes she exaggerates.

Dad dropped off Mom, Amy, Sara, and me at church. Then he took the smiling Jason to pick up Allie Meredith. The rest of us couldn't wait to find out what she looks like!

Fellowship Hall had been transformed. Long tables were covered with checkered tablecloths. Down at one end, near the kitchen, was the food. I hoped someone would bring my favorite beans.

"Where's your father's painting?" Sara asked.

We walked over and stood in front of the fireplace. "When they turn on the lights, you'll be able to see it better!" I told her. Sara had a funny look on her face. "What's wrong?"

"My stockings are falling down!" she said.

"No they aren't!" I said. "You're imagining it. You just aren't used to them yet!"

"Maybe!" Sara said. "But if I'm right, you won't leave me standing here alone, will you?"

"Of course not!" I giggled.

"There she is!" Sara said. "There's Allie Meredith! Standing next to Jason. In the doorway."

"I wish there was more light in here!"

"But candles are more romantic!" Sara said.

"How do you know so much about romance?"

"I don't know. I just do!" Sara said. "Come on! Let's kind of casually walk past, as if we were carrying in a salad or something."

"They'll know we aren't!"

"Then we might spend the entire night wondering what she looks like!" Sara told me.

Frankly, I was afraid Jason would tell me to get lost! But, incredible as it sounds, I don't think my brother even saw me! I looked right at Allie on my way to deliver my imaginary salad.

"Well, what do you think?" I said. "Is she beautiful?"

Sara giggled. "I don't know what I expected. She looks nice, doesn't she?"

I nodded. "I think she's very pretty."

"Pretty, but not beautiful, wouldn't you say?" Sara said.

"That's it!" I agreed. "That's it, exactly."

Sara and I had to sit with my parents during supper. They let Jason and Allie sit at another table. But everytime I looked over, my brother was smiling and talking to Mr. Upjohn.

After dessert, everybody sang some songs. I noticed Sara still doesn't know them.

And then, suddenly, all the lights went out. A spotlight was shining on my father's painting! I could hear people gasp! To be honest, I gasped myself!

"It's beautiful!" Sara said.

"I told you!"

"I never knew your father could paint something as special as that!"

Mr. Upjohn was standing at the microphone. "I am honored to accept this very personal gift from one of the newest members of our congregation," he said. "And now, I'm going to ask Steve Hooper to say a few words."

Everyone was quiet as they watched my father walk to the microphone. "I'm not much for making speeches," he said. "I am very blessed. The Lord has given me talent that lets me re-create what He puts there first! What I paint is the same beauty He gives us all to enjoy every day."

I felt very proud of my father.

"I am honored to be able to share this with

you! My family—Elizabeth, Jason, Katie, and Amy—join me in giving to the Lord a small token of our love for Him!"

I blinked back a tear.

Someone began to sing, "We Love You, Lord!" Everyone joined in. Even Sara!

"You know it!" I whispered.

"I'm learning it," she said. "Thanks to your family, I'm even beginning to understand what the words mean!"

* * * * * * * *

After the dedication of the painting, Sara and I stood off to one side. She told me how much money she had made with her snow blower.

"You're right," I said. "Even with what I made last night, you're still ahead."

"It isn't a race," Sara said. "You showed me that! I just know we'll both get skis!"

I smiled at her. "Sara, I'll have to admit, you certainly had a lot of faith!"

"I did, didn't I!" She grinned. "But, Katie, you had more love!"

* * * * * * * *

Actually, it was a wonderful party! By the time we went home, the Stones had told my par-

141

ents how responsible they think I am. Also, I managed to say "hi" to Allie Meredith without giggling. And Sara's stockings didn't fall down.

In the following days, the Lord didn't reward my family with any special miracles. I couldn't see that we got any more popular! And my father had to borrow money from the bank to pay for the woodburning stove.

But that's OK. As I told Sara before, that wasn't really the point anyhow. Sometimes you just give things out of love!